THE CONSULTANT

A novel by
Claude Bouchard

THE CONSULTANT

Copyright © 1996 by Claude Bouchard

Published by Claude Bouchard

ISBN 978-0-9812790-1-5

Claude Bouchard

Prologue - Tuesday, January 7, 1997

"Who the hell is this?" demanded the voice on the other end of the line.

"Never mind who I am," George replied, his voice a wavering whisper. "Just listen. Quality Imports. Got it? That's all I can say. Quality Imports. Check it out."

He quickly hung up the phone and sat in the darkness of his office, breathing deeply, fighting back the urge to vomit. After a moment, his shaking subsided and the churning in his stomach slowed. He realized that this was dangerous but also knew that he had done the right thing.

Standing, he began to pace back and forth as he continued his deep breathing in an attempt to regain his composure. He started feeling ridiculous and began to relax. There was no reason to worry, he reasoned, he was alone. Anyways, nobody had the slightest idea that he was aware of anything.

Feeling better, he picked up his briefcase and left his office, heading for the main entrance. As he walked by the door leading into the warehouse, he paused then stopped. He had to look again. It was silly because he had seen what he had to see but he felt drawn, as if by some powerful, invisible magnet.

1

He set down his briefcase and, following a moment's hesitation, opened the door.

The warehouse was dark but he had been without light for some time now and his eyes had grown accustomed to its absence. Quickly, he made his way to the rear receiving area where he had seen the cases an hour before.

As he picked up the crowbar he had used earlier and started to pry off the cover of the first wooden case, he could feel the adrenalin pumping through his system once again. The lid came off more easily this time and he leaned it off to one side against the racking. Although this time he knew what to expect, he experienced the same gut wrenching feeling he had felt an hour ago when he had first discovered the cocaine.

At least, he believed it was coke. The shipment came from Columbia and, according to the labels and paperwork, was supposed to be coffee. Though he was far from being a drug expert, he was certain that the contents of this case alone were worth several million dollars on the street.

As he stared in awed horror at the rows of powder filled plastic bags before him, the warehouse lights suddenly came on, bathing the cavernous room in harsh light.

"Good evening, George," a familiar voice greeted from behind him.

He turned to find himself faced by four men, two of whom, like him, were executive managers of the company. The other two, whom he recognized as warehouse employees, were armed with what appeared to be automatic weapons which they pointed directly at him.

"Greg... Wayne... What's going on?" George nervously asked, for lack of something better to say.

"Well," responded Wayne, the company's Director of Operations. "What's going on seems to be that Georgie is not minding his own goddamn business. What do you think, you stupid fuck?"

"Listen," pleaded George, shaking all over again. "Whatever you guys do with your spare time is your own business. Just let me go and I promise I won't say anything. I swear."

"You sure of that, Georgie?" enquired Wayne with a warm smile. "I can't let you go unless you're sure of what you're saying."

"I swear it, Wayne," promised George, sweat streaming from every pore of his body. "I won't say a word. Hell, I'll even quit if you want. I won't even show up tomorrow."

Wayne gazed at him thoughtfully for a few seconds then pulled a handgun equipped with a silencer from under his jacket.

"You got that right, dude," he grinned as he calmly pulled the trigger four times.

"Was that absolutely necessary?" whined Greg, Director of Finance, as George's body slumped to the floor.

"Greg, sometimes I wonder why the fuck I ever involved you in all of this," Wayne snarled in exasperation. "What were we supposed to do? Believe the schmuck and let him go? You just better pray that he didn't speak to anybody about all of this."

Turning to one of the other two, he continued. "Bring his car out back and get him out of here. Dump him and the car in some tough neighbourhood somewhere. Hopefully, the cops will think it was a mugging or something."

"Do you think he might have spoken to somebody?" Greg questioned uneasily as he watched the body being dragged away.

"He can't have been on to us for long so, I doubt it," Wayne replied with his usual overconfidence. "But if he has, I'm sure they'll understand that their best bet is to shut the fuck up."

Chapter 1 - Wednesday, January 8, 1997

Walter Olson signed the last page of the thick, legal-sized document and slid it across the boardroom table to Chris Barry.

Although he knew its contents by heart, Chris allowed himself several minutes to scan the agreement one last time and then also apposed his signature.

The deal was complete. CompuCorp was now majority shareholder of CSS Inc., having acquired all of the shares owned by Walter Olson and Chris Barry.

Founded by Walter Olson some twenty-five years prior, CSS' original *"raison d'être"* had been to offer security and investigative services to the business community at large.

Nine years ago, in a time of difficult markets and falling revenues, Chris Barry, now Executive Vice-President and Chief Operating Officer, had joined the firm and rapidly turned it into a leader in the field of computer security. The company had gone public after three years and had continued to expand ever since. Revenues of the preceding year had slightly exceeded $3 billion and conservative forecasts for the current year were for a 15% increase.

Of the one hundred million outstanding shares, which were currently trading at $16.25, Walter, the firm's president and CEO, held 40%. In addition to a generous salary and a variety of other perks, Walter had awarded Chris with a number of stock options over the years, in recognition of his contribution towards the company's success. Today, this translated in Chris' owning 20% of the firm.

Having turned sixty during the preceding year and satisfied with his accomplishments, Walter had decided that it was time to retire. To ensure a serene retirement, Walter felt it necessary to completely exit the business world and invest his profits in fixed income vehicles, thus eliminating the stress related to the volatility of the stock markets.

His only concern with his decision had been Chris and how the latter would react to it. They had worked extremely well together for nearly a decade and had grown extremely fond of each other during that time.

To Walter's surprise, when he had announced his intentions, Chris had agreed wholeheartedly, even indicating that he also was at a turning point in his life and wished to take it easy for a while and enjoy life with Sandy, his wife.

CSS had been approached with merger propositions on several occasions in recent years and when word had gotten out that the company was for sale, offers had begun pouring in.

Recognizing the firm's current value and future earnings potential, CompuCorp had come in with the best bid, offering CSS shareholders $28 cash per share. Walter and Chris had accepted and were now both much wealthier men.

"Are you sure you won't change your mind, Chris?" asked Jeff Sanders, CEO of CompuCorp. "With Walter out of your hair, you could really make CSS work," he added with a smile.

"Nope," Chris replied without hesitation, shaking his head. "I appreciate the vote of confidence but Walter's the one who really built this company. I just helped keep it profitable over the last few years. He's decided to turn the page and frankly, having worked with him for close to ten years, I really feel that I'm entitled to a well deserved break."

"Do you bastards want me to leave the room so that you can continue your goddamn conversation?" demanded Walter in mock anger, now $470 million richer.

"No, stick around," answered Chris with a smirk. "I'm a rich sonovabitch now and you ain't my boss anymore. I think it's time you heard what I've really got to say about you."

"Unappreciative, little punk," Walter grinned, ending the playful exchange.

"Well, if you change your mind, Chris, let me know," said Sanders. "I have no doubt that we can find a place in our organization for you."

"Thanks," Chris responded. "But thirty-five is not a bad age to retire and I'm sure my wife and I can find something to do to pass the time, at least for a little while."

* * * *

Chris finished collecting the various documents laid out on the boardroom table before him and walked through the door into his spacious adjoining office. Walter, who was already seated in one of the comfortable

7

leather armchairs in the corner and sipping a Chivas, neat, looked up as Chris entered.

"Are you sure this is what you want, kid?" he questioned, not certain if Chris had made the right decision.

"Harry, I'm gonna turn thirty-five in March," Chris patiently replied. "I just signed a contract that will put $560 million in the bank in my name. That's a profit of $235 million with what I consider little or no effort. Yep, this is what I want."

"What are you gonna do now?" pursued Walter, still not convinced.

"To start," laughed Chris. "I'm gonna get a *real* good night's sleep. Then, I will have frequent sex with my wife, which we both thoroughly enjoy, travel, mow the lawn, do crossword puzzles, read and paint. Hell, I might even write a book. That's always been something I wanted to do."

"After that," pressed Walter. "What are you gonna do if you get bored?"

"You worry too much, Walter," Chris chuckled, shrugging his shoulders in exasperation. "After that, if I really get bored, I'll find myself some work to do. You know, freelance. I'll become a consultant."

Chapter 2 - Thursday, January 9, 1997

Employed by the federal government's Ministry of Defence, Jonathan Addley's official title was Director of Police Relations and, although he allotted a small portion of his available time to the duties related to this title, this was not his true function.

He was in fact responsible for a small, yet elite division, the existence of which was known by very few. Though it had no official name, it was sometimes referred to as Discreet Activities and it worked in tight collaboration with similar organizations of other countries. The purpose of this covert network was to supply whatever help it could to ensure the security and well-being of the member countries' citizens.

In so doing, Discreet Activities was open to solving problems at all levels and often dealt with issues that might otherwise be looked after by the police at the municipal, provincial or federal level. In fact, as often was the case, such authorities were actually investigating criminal activities which this clandestine team decided to handle. However, when the division became involved, it always did so without the official knowledge of these law enforcement agencies.

The staff of the Canadian team consisted of little more than a handful of people, carefully recruited by Jonathan. None of them however, were on the government payroll, at least not as salaried civil servants. Rather, when their services were required, they were paid from the government's coffers as consultants.

Their assignments usually consisted of tasks which required high levels of discretion as well as actions that could not be carried out by the customary law enforcement agencies. Each member of the team knew well that in the event of an assignment going sour, their government would not back them up as doing so would be admitting that the network actually existed. They were on their own, but were handsomely compensated for this risk and their efforts.

Though Jonathan did not often recruit new members, he remained constantly on the alert for possible candidates, which were a rare commodity in his line of work. He finished reading the confidential file entitled "Christopher Barry" and leaned back in his chair, reminiscing on how he had come to learn of this new potential recruit.

It had been late morning towards the end of September of the previous year and he had been sitting and chatting in the office of his personal friend and professional ally, Nick Sharp, RCMP Director for the province of Quebec. Nick was one of the few people who were more closely aware of Jonathan's covert activities and the two occasionally helped each other out when possible.

As they had chatted, their conversation had been interrupted by a knock on the door.

"Sorry to bother you, Chief," apologized Arty, one of Nick's officers, coming in and closing the door behind him. "I've got a lady out there who insists on speaking to the person in command."

"What about?" asked Nick.

"Won't say," Arty shrugged. "She just says that she has something of vital importance to discuss with someone high up."

"Of vital importance?" Nick scoffed. "Is she a crazy one?"

They had their share of nuts coming in off the street to supply information about enemy spies with master schemes or aliens from other planets.

"Nope," Arty shook his head. "She's well dressed, good looking, a little agitated, but I don't think she's crazy."

"Alright," Nick sighed. "Show her in."

As Arty left the room Jonathan rose from his seat but Nick waved him back to the chair.

"Stay," he suggested. "Just in case she **is** a wacko, I may need you for protection. Seriously, you're a senior government officer so you can hear what she has to say. Plus, I was hoping you'd buy me lunch so, stick around."

As Jonathan laughed and dropped back into his seat, the door opened once again and Arty entered, followed by an attractive woman in her early thirties. She did seem agitated, her nervousness displayed by her wan smile and her abrupt, rapid movements.

The two men stood to greet her as she moved into the office.

"This is Chief Sharp, ma'am," Arty announced before leaving the room, closing the door on his way out.

"How do you do, Miss...?" enquired Nick, smiling warmly as he extended a hand.

"Mrs." she corrected uncertainly, not responding to the handshake. "Mrs. Denver."

For some reason, the name seemed vaguely familiar.

"Well, Mrs. Denver, I'm Nick Sharp and this is Jonathan Addley," said Nick as he sat back down. "Mr. Addley's with the Ministry of Defence. Have a seat, please."

As she lowered herself into an armchair, she eyed Jonathan suspiciously and asked, "Does he have to be here?"

"I was told that you wished to speak to somebody high up," answered Nick with a serious smile. "Mr. Addley is about as high up as they get. You have nothing to worry about."

"O.K." she hesitantly replied. "I just want to be careful with who I talk to."

"Quite understandable," Nick replied soothingly, wondering if she **was** mentally imbalanced. "Now, how can we help you Mrs. Denver?"

She stared at both men, the uncertainty clear in her eyes, then took a deep breath and spoke.

"Before I say anything, I want you to promise me immunity and, if required, protection."

"Immunity and protection from what?" queried Nick, his curiosity mounting.

"What I have to talk about concerns a major murder case in Montreal, which was solved a couple of months ago," she responded, hesitating before adding, "The killer is still on the loose."

Nick leaned forward slightly in his chair. Denver; the name became more familiar although he still couldn't pinpoint exactly why. Maybe this lady wasn't crazy after all.

"What killer, ma'am," he asked softly.

"Immunity and protection," she insisted, a little more confident. "Then I'll talk."

Nick glanced at Jonathan who gave a slight nod. He was also curious as to what this lady had to say.

"O.K. Mrs. Denver," Nick accepted. "I'll presume that you aren't guilty of some hideous crime and, on that basis, I'll agree to your request. However, until you tell us more, I can't promise you anything specific."

"I haven't really done anything wrong myself," she nervously explained. "M-my late husband did some things with computers though, that I was aware of. That's the extent of my guilt."

"Well, that sounds tame enough," reassured Nick. "I'm sure we can overlook that in exchange for something concrete about a murder."

"Murders," she corrected. "Alright, I'm going to trust you gentlemen. Frankly, I've got nothing to lose, nowhere to go and I'm scared as hell."

She took a deep breath to calm herself and plunged ahead. "Are you familiar with the Vigilante?"

Denver... Carl Denver... It all came back to Nick. Two months earlier, Carl Denver had committed suicide when cornered by the police. For a period of seven months, the Vigilante had been active in the Montreal area, killing a variety of criminals which the system had either failed to penalize or never caught up with. Approximately thirty victims had met their fate before the authorities had finally zeroed in on Denver.

From what Nick could remember, the evidence in that case had been airtight. Denver was the Vigilante and he was dead. His wife had disappeared on the day of his death.

"You are Mrs. Carl Denver?" Nick stated more than asked, staring at the woman before him.

"Yes," she replied with pride. "And my husband was innocent. Carl never hurt anybody. He hated violence."

"Mrs. Denver, I realize that this is difficult for you to accept," Nick sceptically insisted. "But from what I know about the Vigilante case, the evidence was rather clear. One of the murder weapons, a blood stained baseball bat, was found in your husband's car. Blood tests matched with some of the victims. Computer records showed that he had sent and erased messages to the police on Eazy-Com."

"Carl was framed," she retorted emphatically.

"Then why did he kill himself when the cops went to him?" Nick shot back.

"The money," she quietly replied.

"What money?" asked Nick, somewhat puzzled.

He did not remember anything about money being involved in the Vigilante case.

"Carl was a computer genius," Mrs. Denver replied, less proud. "He had been skimming money from a variety of sources for a while; banks, trusts, brokers, that kind of thing. On the day that he died, we were planning to disappear. I did. He died. We had six million dollars accumulated in an account in the Cayman Islands."

"So you're saying," Nick spoke slowly, "That your husband killed himself because he thought he was getting busted for the money scams?"

"That's the only thing that makes sense," she nodded, tears welling up. "Carl was not the Vigilante. He rarely went out alone and we were together on many of the nights that murders took place. On several occasions, we were even out to dinner. Credit card slips were signed by Carl. Check it out. You'll see Carl was not the killer."

"Do you have any idea who the killer might be?" Nick gently enquired.

"No, not really," Mrs. Denver shook her head. "It was someone who discovered what Carl was doing with the money, but I don't know who."

"How do you know that?" probed Nick.

"Carl and I had agreed that, no matter what, I was to take the plane and leave. I did and made it to the Caymans. When I tried to access the cash, the account had been cleaned out. The killer is still out there, my husband is dead, I'm broke and wanted by the cops. I'm scared, gentlemen. I will do what I can to help you but you must help me."

"We're going to have to check all of this out, you understand," Nick informed her. "But if what you're telling us is true, yes, we will help you, Mrs. Denver. We have a witness protection programme we can get you into. You have nothing to worry about."

"What happens now?" she asked helplessly. "I had left, and returned, under an assumed name. I don't have anywhere to go and like I said, I'm broke. The only money I do have is in the bank under my real name. I'm not real comfortable in going there or going back home."

"And we wouldn't want you to do that either," answered Nick. "We have a few places, safe-houses, where we keep witnesses from time to time. We'll set you up there until we can work things out. Don't worry, you'll be comfortable and in complete security."

He picked up the phone and punched a few numbers. "Arty, we have a guest here for our Lake Brome residence. I'd like you and Sammy to drive her down there. Thanks."

He replaced the receiver in its cradle and smiled at Mrs. Carl Denver. "We're all set. All you have to do now is relax and let us do our job. I'll let you know if you can do anything else to help."

"Thank-you," she murmured gratefully and rose to her feet as Arty opened the office door to escort her out.

Once she had gone, Nick glanced at Jonathan and feigning surprise, exclaimed, "Oh, are you still here?"

Grinning, Jonathan replied, "Yep. Just didn't have much to say. You asked all the right questions so why should I interrupt?"

"So? What do you think?" asked Nick.

The lady's story had been quite believable but he didn't know quite what to make of it.

"I think she's telling the truth," Jonathan answered with conviction. "Once we start checking, everything will pan out."

"We?" enquired Nick, now his turn to grin.

Smiling widely, Jonathan replied, "You know how my mind works, Nick. I followed the Vigilante case closely enough and was pretty impressed by the guy. Honestly, I was disappointed when it ended. Not because they had caught up with him, mind you, although I did consider the man was actually doing society a favour. What really bothered me was that he ended up not being as smart as I had given him credit for. Now, to find out that he's not gone, it's not over, that he got away clean as a whistle? Now, I'm proud of him again."

"So, you're thinking recruit?" asked Nick, although it was not really a question.

"You never know," Jonathan admitted. "Let me work on this for a bit and save you some man-hours."

"Be my guest," Nick invited. "I much prefer spending your budget over mine."

16

"Speaking of which," replied Addley. "I believe that I'm supposed to buy you lunch. Let's go."

During the months which had followed the initial meeting with Mrs. Denver, Jonathan, with the help of a few consultants, had quietly begun digging into the Vigilante case. They had been quickly able to confirm that Carl Denver's wife had spoken the truth as Carl's whereabouts could be clearly established on many occasions when murders had taken place.

This had led Jonathan to review the entire Vigilante investigation with two major questions in mind. Who was the actual killer, and why had the money which Denver had electronically skimmed never been questioned, never even been an issue?

As Jonathan had continued to search for answers, one name had strangely kept popping up; Chris Barry, Executive Vice President at CSS, Denver's employer. Barry had worked closely with the police on the case and, by monitoring Denver's PC activities, had been the one to discover the latter's Eazy-Com message transmissions and subsequent erasures. If this was actually what had transpired, why hadn't Carl's money scams been uncovered? These had all been accomplished with the use of the computer, hadn't they? And according to Mrs. Denver, Carl had performed several of his tricks during the weeks which had preceded his death. Police records indicated that Barry had been monitoring Denver's PC during that period of time.

Verification of Barry's financial records had confirmed that he had not taken the cash unless it had been diverted to some confidential account. This, Jonathan doubted as the guy was filthy rich as it was. It was not as if he needed an additional six million.

The investigation reports had mentioned the possible involvement of a mini-van in the Vigilante crimes and Carl Denver owned a Chevy Astro. Interestingly enough, although this was far from solid evidence, DMV records indicated that Barry had owned a Chrysler Town & Country at the time. In addition, though it had no bearing in the case, both men had coincidentally also owned Corvettes. Barry had since replaced both vehicles.

It was when Jonathan decided to look into the past that things, however still fragmented and inconclusive, became more promising. Through birth records, he had come to discover the identity of Barry's parents.

His father had died when Chris was very young, leaving Mrs. Barry to see to the upbringing of her son and daughter, alone. She had taken on employment as a cashier with a major supermarket chain where she had remained until a few years ago, when she had retired. Group insurance records indicated a Jean Picard, common-law spouse, as her beneficiary, a number of years earlier.

When attempting to establish the whereabouts of Mr. Picard, Jonathan had learned that the gentleman had been murdered a few months prior, the time of death coinciding with the end of the Vigilante's activities. Police records indicated that Picard had had a history of domestic violence which included complaints submitted by Mrs. Barry. She had eventually left the man, bless her heart.

The past of Chris Barry's wife, Cassandra Taylor, had also proved somewhat interesting. At the age of seventeen, she had witnessed the murder of her father during a fouled hold-up at the family-owned convenience store. Those responsible, three unidentified teenagers, had never been caught. As chance would have it, Cassandra and Carl Denver had both grown up in the same neighbourhood and, although she was a couple of years older than he, both had attended the same high school.

Jonathan had paid Carl's mother a visit to try to find out more about the supposed Vigilante and his earlier years. He had heard her speak of a quiet, studious boy, beyond reproach, except for those hoodlum friends of his, Mike and Eddy. When he had later attempted to track these gentlemen down, Jonathan had discovered that both had since been murdered, one as recently as last July, in Vancouver. Verification had quickly shown that Barry, as well as Denver, had been on the West Coast at the time.

Jonathan knew that he did not have anything close to a foolproof case against Chris Barry. In fact, what he had was really nothing more than a lot of bits and pieces which could all be attributed to coincidence. However, he also had a gut feeling and such feelings had proven more often right than wrong in the past.

He had just learned that Mr. Barry had recently opted for a very early retirement, having sold his interest in CSS Inc. Considering that the gentleman was about to have much more free time on his hands, Jonathan felt that the time was right to get together with Chris to discuss the past and, possibly, the future.

Chapter 3 - Friday, January 10, 1997

Officer John Riley turned right off De Lorimier onto Logan and immediately saw the turquoise Plymouth Sundance, still parked in the same spot.

He had first noticed the vehicle two days earlier and had written a ticket for parking by a fire hydrant. The previous day, he had seen the car again and called in the plate number to verify if it was stolen, which it wasn't. He had added a second parking ticket to the first.

He pulled up behind the automobile and climbed out of the warmth of his cruiser to investigate further. Although the abandoned car's windows were somewhat frosted from the cold, he could see inside well enough and noted nothing of interest. The parking tickets remained in place under the wiper blade, indicating that the vehicle had not yet been moved. He tried the doors but both were locked, as was the trunk. Returning to his patrol car, he called in to dispatch.

"Kelly? Riley. Listen, you want to check on plate number TIN 147? Turquoise Plymouth Sundance, a couple of years old. I'd like a name and address of ownership. The car's been abandoned. Let me know when you find something. In the meantime, send a tow truck to the corner of Logan and De

Lorimier to pick this thing up cuz it's been here for over two days. Thanks. Over."

As he set down the transmitter, he gazed at the abandoned car and suddenly noticed something which he had not earlier. Several brownish-red, elongated spots could be seen on the license plate, as if someone had splashed a few drops of paint or stain.

Climbing back out into the bitter cold, he hurried over to get a closer look and, though he wasn't certain, those stains could be blood. Several more similar spots were splattered on the car's bumper.

Determined to find out more, he went to the trunk of his cruiser and pulled out a crowbar. Returning to the Plymouth, he jammed one end of the crowbar under the lid of the trunk and, with the help of his two hundred fourteen pounds, popped the trunk open like a bottle top.

The body inside was frozen solid, thanks to Montreal's sub-zero January weather. He searched the corpse for identification and quickly found a wallet in an inside pocket of the man's suit jacket. As he looked into the wallet for I.D., the portable transmitter-receiver attached to his coat collar crackled.

"52-10, do you read me?" called Kelly's voice.

"Yeah," Riley grimly replied. "I read you."

"I've got that ownership information you wanted on the Sundance."

"Let me guess," interrupted Riley, "George Robinson, 6240 Rosemont Boulevard."

"That's right," responded Kelly. "How did you know?"

"I found his driver's permit in his wallet," answered Riley. "I asked for a tow truck before. You better send a meat wagon too because this guy's definitely dead."

Chapter 4 - Monday, January 13, 1997

Chris Barry sat at the large crescent-shaped desk in his corner office on the twelfth floor of the CSS building. It was a sunny day and he was admiring the view, watching the sun's reflections as they bounced off the expanse of snow covered ground and trees in Maisonneuve Park across the street below.

He knew that he would miss this place but he was due for a well earned break. He estimated that he had put in excess of thirty-five thousand hours in the rebuilding of this company over the last nine years and felt he now deserved some free time to truly enjoy life with his precious Sandy. Vacations over the years had always been interrupted on a daily basis with phone calls, faxes and decisions to be made. It would be nice to travel with only leisure activities in mind for a change.

The buzz of the intercom broke into his reverie.

"Chris, there's a Jonathan Addley down at the gate who wants to see you. Says he's with the Ministry of Defence. Steve says the I.D. looks official."

"O.K. Sonia," replied Chris. "Let him in. I'll see him."

A visitor would be a nice break in the monotony as this was Chris' last week and he didn't really have much to do. The people from CompuCorp had collected pretty much all the files of current and potential contracts, leaving Chris and Walter with little to occupy their final hours with the firm.

Following several minutes of waiting, the intercom buzzed again.

"Mr. Barry, Mr. Addley is here to see you," Sonia's voice formally announced.

"Thanks," Chris acknowledged. "Be right there."

He crossed the wide expanse of white oak flooring to the door leading to the tasteful reception area which also served as Sonia's office.

Seated in one of the comfortable visitors chairs was a man in his early forties who did not resemble any of the government bureaucrats Chris had met in the past. Of medium height and build, this man looked fit, tough and determined. Chris had a strange impression that his visitor would have felt right at home in a camouflage suit, tracking enemy snipers in a jungle somewhere. As he approached, he had a weird feeling that his guest was sizing him.

"Mr. Addley," greeted Chris with his usual charming smile.

"Mr. Barry." Jonathan jovially responded, standing as he reached for his host's extended hand.

"Can I offer you something to drink?" offered Chris, gracious as always.

"If you can find a cup of coffee somewhere, that would be great," accepted Jonathan.

Chris glanced at an already nodding Sonia and grinned. He would definitely miss her once he was gone. She deserved to have her picture by the definition of 'Administrative Assistant Extraordinaire' in any dictionary.

"What can I do for you?" Chris curiously enquired, ushering his guest into his office.

"I was hoping you and I could discuss a little business," answered Jonathan as Chris gestured for him to sit.

"You might not be aware of this, Mr. Addley, but CSS has been sold to CompuCorp. I will be leaving the company at the end of the week so I'm probably not the best person to speak to. Perhaps I can refer you to someone over there?"

"No, Mr. Barry," Jonathan confidently replied. "You really are the person that I want to speak to."

"Sure, fine," Chris shrugged. "And call me Chris. Formality and I don't get along very well."

"O.K., Chris it is," smiled Addley. "You can call me Jonathan."

They paused for a moment as Sonia entered the room with a complete coffee service. Once she had gone, Chris did the honours and they resumed their conversation.

"Now then, back to my original question. What can I do for you?" Chris asked.

Jonathan eyed Chris intently for a moment before answering. His in-depth study of the man over the last three months had clearly indicated that Chris Barry was a highly intelligent man and this first personal contact did not lead Jonathan to believe any differently. It was in Barry's eyes; blue as ice; intense, brilliant eyes. Jonathan sensed that Chris was not one with whom to play games. His best bet was to play it straight; sort of.

"Chris, I'm gonna tell you a story that I'm putting together," Jonathan started. "Maybe it's fiction, maybe not. I don't know. I'd like you to listen to the story and when I'm done, we can discuss it if you wish. Sound fair?"

"Hey, it's not like CompuCorp left me with a whole lot to do," laughed Chris. "I've got time. Tell me a story."

24

"O.K. Here it goes," Jonathan went on. "There's this kid who's brought up surrounded by violence in the streets and at home. He's a smart kid and grows up to be very successful. But the violence he saw and endured during his younger years left him with scars that he has to deal with."

He paused for a sip of coffee then continued.

"To add to his pain, the young lady he has married was witness to her father's murder. The only way he finds to help the healing process is through violent acts of vengeance. He therefore becomes the Vigilante and makes people pay for their crimes."

"Interesting," Chris nodded approvingly. "Go on."

"Being a very intelligent and calculating man, our man plans his deeds well and never gets caught, never leaves a trace. He doesn't intend to go on forever, but he must ease the hurt. Most of his victims are personally unknown to him and are simply part of his therapy. But there are a few people, four to be exact, who must die for the healing to be complete. Three of them are those have caused personal pain to his wife by taking the life of her father. Able to identify them, her decision at the time was to make them pay some day herself. As destiny would have it, she has since married our hero, who is willing and able to handle this task for her. Two of these individuals die. The third is reserved for later."

Jonathan went for another sip of coffee, watching Chris closely for any signs of stress. Detecting nothing of the sort, he pressed on.

"The fourth person is his mother's lover from many years before. This man's crime is not obvious but it probably relates to domestic violence. His death is justified and necessary for our hero to complete the healing process."

"So our man kills his mother's ex-lover?" Chris requested clarification.

"That's right," Jonathan nodded. "We now come back to the third murderer of our man's father-in-law. Planned or destiny, I don't know, but he ends up employed by none other than our hero. In the end, this poor soul is framed for the rash of murders and commits suicide, leaving everyone to believe that the Vigilante is dead. What do you think of my story, Chris?"

"It's an incredible story, Jonathan," Chris admitted, impressed. "It is violent at times but it has a happy ending. *Is* this a true story, Jonathan?"

Jonathan eyed his host intently as the latter spoke, searching for signs of nervousness or panic. What he saw however, was a calm man, definitely relaxed and composed.

"Quite frankly, like I said, I don't know," answered Jonathan. "What do you think, Chris?"

"It could be true," Chris reasoned. "It definitely sounds plausible. Is that where the story ends or does something else happen?"

Although he really had nothing more to base himself on, Jonathan was now convinced that Chris Barry was the Vigilante. Why else would the man have listened to him and be willing to pursue this strange conversation. He had to make a decision, as he had done in the past with other recruits. Was Barry stable enough to warrant continuing the process or was he some psychopath presently in remission? Jonathan gazed thoughtfully at Chris for a moment and decided that this was probably the most solid candidate he had ever interviewed. He could continue.

"There is more to the story, Chris," Jonathan replied. "A witness comes forward, claiming the innocence of the dead, supposed Vigilante. This brings a special agent to discreetly investigate the case all over again and he discovers that what the witness says is true. Many of the murders occurred while the supposed Vigilante's presence could be vouched for elsewhere. The agent continues to dig and eventually finds the person he believes to be the true Vigilante who, of course, is alive and well."

Chris smiled, thoroughly entertained. "This really is a great story, Jonathan. What happens next?"

"The agent meets with the Vigilante. Now, you must understand that the agent heads an obscure department of the government, which is unknown to the public. This department is responsible for what we might call clandestine activities aimed at the betterment of the country and its allies."

"Wow. Isn't that a very important person to have investigating a local murder case?" asked Chris, amused, "Especially a case which is already officially solved?"

"Well, the agent's objective is not to catch the Vigilante," explained Jonathan with a smile. "The agent is responsible for recruiting new members for this secret department."

"Sure, that makes sense," chuckled Chris. "Jonathan, this is great. Are you telling me that the agent wants to hire the Vigilante to work for the government?"

"The agent is impressed with the Vigilante and believes that his talents could be a definite asset to his department and to the country."

"But what if the Vigilante is not interested?" enquired Chris, suddenly pensive. "What happens then?"

"Nothing," Jonathan replied. "Disappointed, the agent goes away to find recruits elsewhere."

"What about blackmail?" Chris probed on, "Any chance that this agent might try that route with the Vigilante? You know, to convince him to join the team?"

"Not worth it," Addley shook his head. "Those who join the team must be fully devoted. Also, as I mentioned, very few are aware of this department's existence so the agent couldn't just come forward to make the Vigilante story public. Doing so might put the department's secrecy at risk."

Chris nodded thoughtfully and asked, "What about the witness? Couldn't the witness try to make the whole thing public?"

Again, Addley shook his head as he replied, "All that the witness needs to be told is that following an investigation, the authorities were unable to discover the true identity of the Vigilante. To ensure her safety however, she will be kept in the witness protection programme indefinitely."

She... No doubt Carl's wife, thought Chris.

He smiled as he spoke, "And you're certain that she will keep quiet?"

"She has no idea who the true Vigilante is," Jonathan answered, realizing his slip-up, too late. "All she knows is that he is not dead. She will keep quiet. Her main concern is physical and financial survival. That will be supplied."

"Well, Jonathan," said Chris, standing to indicate the end of their meeting. "I like your story. It's got promise."

"Thanks, Chris," Jonathan replied, also rising to his feet. "Listen, would you mind thinking about the story for a bit and giving me a call. I haven't nailed down where it will go from here. Maybe you can make some suggestions?"

He pulled a card from his jacket pocket which he handed to Chris. All that appeared on the card was a telephone number.

"I'll think about it," Chris nodded. "I'm about to have a lot of free time on my hands so, who knows? Maybe I can help you out."

"Excellent. I'm sure you could be really helpful," said Jonathan. "Sir, I appreciate your hospitality and, hopefully, we'll be talking soon."

He shook his host's hand and then headed for the exit. As he reached the door, he stopped and turned.

"By the way, Chris, that witness who came forward; would you think that she could be in any danger?"

"Nah, I doubt it," Chris replied with a reassuring smile. "From what you told me, she doesn't really know anything and hasn't done anything wrong. I'm sure that she's not in any danger whatsoever."

* * * *

Nick Sharp was scanning through the New Activity Report which the computer spewed out on a daily basis. The report was a compilation of data entered into the National Police Information Network by officers at the local, provincial and federal levels and contained thousands of pieces of information regarding new cases, leads on open cases and solved cases. Though information regarding cases anywhere in Canada was available on request, the system was programmed to automatically generate only data related to cases within a geographic area defined for a specific RCMP division. For Nick, this represented the province of Quebec.

As he glanced through the pages, he happened upon a name which seemed familiar; Quality Imports. Quickly, he read the details of the new case, a murder which was being investigated by the Montreal police; body found in the trunk of a car; shot four times in the chest; victim's name, George Robinson; age thirty-one; five-seven, one hundred fifty-eight pounds; male, Caucasian, brown hair and eyes, single; Director, M.I.S. for Quality Imports.

He picked up the phone and punched in a few numbers. "Arty, remember that call you got last week? Some guy was telling you to check out some company? Yeah, that's the one. What was the name of the company? Quality Imports? Are you sure? Well, I'm just going through the Activity Report and it seems that the locals found a body on Friday, in the trunk of a car. The guy's been identified as George Robinson, employed by Quality Imports. Yup, strange coincidence. No, that's all right. Let me make a few calls. I'll let you know if I need anything else."

Chapter 5 - Tuesday, January 14, 1997

As Jonathan Addley climbed into his comfortable, government supplied automobile the cell phone in the breast pocket of his jacket started to vibrate.

"Yeah," he spoke into the phone as he closed the door and started the engine.

"How's it going, bud?" enquired Nick Sharp's familiar voice.

"Hang on a second," replied Jonathan, pausing to activate the scrambler system. One could never be too careful with cell phones. "O.K., I've got the scrambler going now. To answer your question, it's going pretty good. What's up?"

"Jon, we got a call last Tuesday, anonymous, telling us to check out Quality Imports, some import firm in the Laval industrial park. Arty, who got the call, brought it to my attention and did some routine checks on their financial status, customers, bank records, that sort of thing. Everything looked kosher. Now, yesterday, I'm going over the New Activity Report and there's this new murder the locals are looking into. Victim turns out to be the M.I.S. Director for Quality Imports. The preliminary M.E. report this morning estimates the time of death as somewhere between last Tuesday night and Wednesday morning."

"Interesting coincidence," replied Jonathan thoughtfully as he drove amidst the morning traffic. "What can I do to help?"

"Well, I've got a feeling that the call Arty got and this murder are related. But, we can't just go busting in there, we have no grounds to do so. Neither would the municipal police if I told them about this. I was wondering if this might be a little project you'd want to think about. Maybe you can get one of your snoops in there, just to look around."

"The guy was in charge of M.I.S.?" asked Jonathan, his ever-active mind switching to a higher gear.

"Yup. That's what the report says," Nick answered.

"O.K. Let me think about it. I have a possible new recruit who happens to be somewhat knowledgeable with computers. This might be a good testing ground for him if he's interested. Leave it with me. I'll get back to you."

* * * *

"CSS, Good afternoon."

"Good afternoon," said Jonathan. "Chris Barry, please."

"I'm sorry, sir. Mr. Barry is no longer in our employment," the receptionist sadly replied.

"Oh really? I thought he was remaining until the end of the week?"

"Well, technically, he is, sir," the receptionist informed him. "But he has decided to take the last few days off."

"I see," responded Jonathan. "Can you put me through to his secretary?"

"One moment, sir."

He waited as the connection was made and, following a couple of rings, someone responded.

"Chris Barry's office, Sonia speaking."

"Good afternoon, Sonia. Jonathan Addley. I met with Mr. Barry yesterday morning."

"Yes, Mr. Addley. How are you?"

"Fine, thanks. I understand that Chris decided to leave early?"

"Yes, unfortunately," Sonia confirmed.

"I discussed a project of possible interest with Chris when we met and he's supposed to get back to me. However, I may need his help sooner than I had originally anticipated so I'd have to speak to him. Do you know if I can reach him at home?"

"I don't think so," Sonia answered carefully, always the discreet secretary. "I believe he and his wife went skiing for a few days."

"Do you happen to know where?" Jonathan hopefully enquired.

"Unfortunately not," replied Sonia.

"O.K. Thanks for your help. If Chris calls, can you ask him to get in touch with me as soon as possible? He has my number."

"Absolutely, Mr. Addley."

"Thanks, Sonia. Bye."

Jonathan cut the connection and punched in a few numbers. "Hi, Shirley. Jonathan. I'm looking for a Chris Barry who's gone skiing for a couple of days. I'm presuming he's stayed relatively local. Can you try to get a handle on where he might be and let me know? I need to speak to the gentleman. No, don't leave a message. Just let me know where he is if you find him. Thanks."

Shirley Tompkins was responsible for all travel and lodging arrangements for the personnel of the Ministry of Defence and she was an ace. If Chris Barry was booked in a hotel or resort somewhere, anywhere, she would find him.

Chapter 6 - Wednesday, January 15, 1997

Chris reached the bottom of the slope, coming expertly to a halt, and turned to watch Sandy finish her descent. It was hard to believe that this was only her second season; she skied like a pro. But then again, she had had the opportunity to practice.

Her school schedule last winter had been such that she had no classes on Mondays and Fridays and, after her first taste of skiing, she had quickly fallen into the habit of getting her studies out of the way by Sunday. This had allowed her additional practice of the sport for fifteen consecutive Mondays the previous year.

She approached him at a rapid pace, stopping at the last moment and making sure to spray him considerably with the snow from her skis in the process.

"Sorry," she apologized with an impish grin as she leaned over to kiss him.

"Yeah, right," he laughed, wiping snow from his cheek with a gloved hand. "Want to go for a last run?"

"I think I'd rather call it a day," she prudently decided. "This **is** our first time this year and I'm already under the impression that I'm gonna hurt tomorrow."

"Chicken," her husband taunted with a smile.

"Yup," agreed Sandy. "Go on, tough guy. Just don't complain tomorrow when you wake up stiff all over. I'll go take a shower and limber up. Meet you in the bar in forty-five minutes?"

"Deal," he said, kissing her again before heading off to the chair-lift.

As he approached the chairs, he reasoned that he too was starting to experience some muscular pain.

"Maybe she's right," he thought. "Shouldn't overdo it. We will be here for another two days."

He changed direction and headed for the lodge where the bar was located, a cold rum and coke being his next objective. After shedding his skis and poles, he entered the cozy bar and made his way to a small table by the fireplace. Within moments, he was comfortably seated, contently sipping his objective.

"How are you, Chris?" a vaguely familiar voice asked from behind him.

He turned towards the voice and smiled in surprise at the man standing there.

"Jonathan. What a pleasant surprise. Have a seat."

"Well, I don't want to barge in on you," Addley politely replied.

"Come on. Have a seat," Chris insisted, pushing a chair back with his foot. "You didn't go to the trouble of finding me just to say hello, did you?"

"Guess not," Jonathan grinned as he settled into the chair.

"So what's up?" queried Chris, leaning back comfortably.

"I was wondering if you had a chance to think about the story we discussed?"

"Yeah, a little," Chris nodded. "The way I see it, your hero might be interested in the agent's proposition. His wife however, is not sure if he should do it or not."

"I see," replied Jonathan, his expression thoughtful. "Say an opportunity came up for our hero to try his hand at this new line of work. A little job that would probably turn into nothing, a testing ground, so to speak. Do you think he might be willing to give it a shot?"

"I'd say it would depend on what exactly the job was," Chris answered, obviously interested. "Have you determined that?"

"In fact, I have," admitted Jonathan. "Let's say the cops get a call, anonymous, telling them to look into a company. Let's call it Quality Imports. Shortly after, a man is found dead in the trunk of his car. He turns out to be the M.I.S. manager for the very same company. Now our hero, who happens to be a computer wizard, offers his services to this firm. They're in need of a computer guy and he has a reputation for being the best. They accept his services and he's in. Once inside, he can snoop around to see if anything wrong is going on."

"That's it?" exclaimed Chris, nodding approvingly. "I think that would work, Jonathan. Our hero could probably convince his wife to agree to his doing something like that."

"Good," said Jonathan. "One thing I don't believe I had pointed out when we spoke the other day. Due to the sensitive nature of the activities carried out, our hero would have no official government backing. Only a handful of people know that this department even exists."

"So if our hero gets caught doing something nasty, he's on his own?" Chris slowly suggested.

"That's right," Addley explained. "In the sense that no government official would step in and say, 'It's O.K., he was working for us'. Now, this doesn't mean that no support is available to our hero if he found himself in a jam. I should also mention that he would be handsomely compensated in return for this element of risk."

Chris considered this for a moment before replying. "As long as our hero is aware of these conditions, no problem."

"Excellent," said Jonathan, rising to his feet. "You're really helping me with my story. I'll be in touch."

As he turned to leave, he stopped and looked at Chris. "By the way, remember the guy who was framed as the Vigilante? Say he had embezzled a large amount of money. What do you think would have happened to that money afterwards?"

Chris shrugged with a grin. "I don't know. How about if it was transferred by our hero to a number of worthwhile charities?"

"I like it," Jonathan chuckled. "We'll go with that."

"Who was that?" questioned Sandy, motioning towards the departing man as she joined her husband at the table.

"That, my dear, was my new friend, Jonathan," Chris replied.

"Coincidence?" she asked.

"Nah," Chris shook his head. "The world ain't that small. He tracked me down to offer me a trial run. Just to see if I'd like this kind of work."

"I don't know, Chris," Sandy worriedly replied. "This could be dangerous."

"It could," he admitted. "But somebody's got to do it."

"But does it have to be you?"

38

"It doesn't have to be," Chris quietly responded. "But it could."

"You want to do this, don't you?" said Sandy, more a statement than a question.

"It seems intriguing, that's for sure," Chris acknowledged.

"How well does it pay?" Sandy asked.

Chris laughed as he replied. "Apparently well, but I don't know specifically. Would that really make a difference considering our financial situation?"

She shrugged and was silent for a moment. "You promise you'll be careful?"

"All the time," he reassured her. "Now, let's enjoy our vacation. It seems that I'm going back to work soon."

Chapter 7 - Monday, January 20, 1997

Although almost two weeks had gone by since George Robinson had died, Charles Peterson, owner and president of Quality Imports, was still shaken by his M.I.S. Director's tragic end.

George had been with the company almost since it had been founded ten years earlier so, not only had Charles lost a friend, he had also lost the only person who knew the entire systems layout. Never having developed the slightest interest for computers, Peterson had always counted fully on Robinson, who had literally built the firm's information systems. The two programmers and computer operator were doing their best to keep up with the workload but George had been a hands-on manager and the true backbone of the M.I.S. department. Charles knew that he had to find a solid replacement quickly but had no idea what he was even looking for.

A knock on the door brought him out of his miserable reverie.

"Mr. Peterson, there's a Mr. Chris Barry at the reception area who would like to see you," announced Crystal, his secretary. "He says he can help us with our M.I.S. problems."

Chris Barry. The name sounded familiar.

"Did he say where he's from?" asked Peterson, trying to remember where he had heard the name before.

"He says he was with CSS until the recent takeover by CompuCorp," Crystal replied.

That's why the name rang a bell. He had read about the acquisition in the papers. Barry was the guy who had put CSS on the map.

"Sure, Crystal," Peterson responded, suddenly curious and excited. "I'll see him. Send him in."

While he waited for his visitor to arrive, he pondered as to why Barry was here to see him in the first place. For one, no recruiting activities had yet been initiated; getting over the shock of George's murder had required some time. Secondly, Barry was a king in the world of business. Why would such a man be interested in helping a small firm like Quality Imports? He could have stayed with CompuCorp and become CEO within a couple of years but, according to the papers, Barry had refused to remain with the company, opting for a very early retirement instead.

The door opened and Crystal ushered their visitor in.

"Mr. Peterson, pleasure to meet you," greeted Chris with his usual charm.

"The pleasure's all mine, Mr. Barry. Please have a seat. Coffee?'

"No, thanks," Chris declined. "But you go ahead if you want some."

"I have enough to keep me up nights without adding caffeine to the mix," replied Peterson with a wan smile.

He nodded to his secretary who left the office, closing the door behind her.

"I understand that you're here to offer your services, Mr. Barry?" Peterson continued. "Frankly, I'm flattered but also a little puzzled, a man of your stature."

Chris smiled and explained. "I've been on a diet of eighty hours of work per week for the last ten years. I felt I needed a break so my initial intention was to stop working when our company was acquired. I presume you've heard about the CSS acquisition?"

Peterson nodded and Chris went on.

"Now, I've come to realize that you don't put in eighty hours per week unless you enjoy working. This being the case, I've also realized that quitting cold turkey is a lot harder than I thought it would be. Therefore, in order to allow myself a less painful withdrawal, I've decided to offer my services on a contract basis to whoever might be interested."

"O.K. I understand that part," acknowledged Peterson. "Now, could you explain what suddenly brings you to my doorstep?"

Chris took on a more serious air as he answered, "I have a few friends who are with the police and one of them told me about your M.I.S. Manager's untimely death. I saw a possible opportunity for the two of us to help each other to our mutual benefit. I hope that doesn't sound too cold or disrespectful."

"I guess not," Peterson shrugged his shoulders. "I mean, you didn't know George so it makes it much easier for you to look at the whole thing from a business perspective. And, I definitely do need help with my computer department. I don't know or understand a damn thing in that area. George put together all of our systems; accounting, payroll, inventory control, everything. The problem is that documentation wasn't George's strong point. He had everything in his head."

"Well, I'd be open to analyzing your systems and putting together the documentation for you," offered Chris. "Like I said, I'm looking for a little contractual work, not a full time job. While I do that, you could look for a full time replacement. I could also help you with the technical side of the recruiting if you want."

"I guess I'd be a fool to refuse," Peterson nodded thoughtfully. "I'm just not sure that I can afford you, Mr. Barry, a man of your expertise."

"Don't believe everything you read in the papers," Chris warned with a grin. "I'm not that good. Make me an offer, Charlie. I'm not doing this to get rich."

"Seventy-five hundred a month?" suggested Peterson hopefully.

"That's fine," Chris replied.

"Then we've got a deal, Mr. Barry," Peterson exclaimed, extending his hand as he stood.

"Great," said Chris as he rose to shake Peterson's hand. "One last thing. You'll have to drop the 'Mr. Barry' stuff and call me Chris. I don't function well under formality."

"Sure, Chris," Peterson agreed. "And you can call me Charlie."

Chris grinned, "I already did."

* * * *

Having agreed to assume his duties the following morning, Chris drove his new Pathfinder out of the Quality Imports parking lot and, within minutes, was cruising eastbound on the 440, away from Laval's industrial park. He picked up his cellular phone and punched in the most recent speed dial number he had created.

"Hello," answered a voice after two rings.

"Good morning," greeted Chris. "This is your co-author."

"Hang on a second," replied Jonathan, activating the scrambler. "O.K. We can talk now. What's up?"

"Just wanted to tell you that there's been some progress with our story," Chris announced. "Our hero has managed to obtain temporary employment with that firm we had talked about."

"Excellent," exclaimed an impressed Jonathan. "When would he start?"

"I figure we might as well have him start tomorrow," Chris replied.

"That soon? That's great. Let me know how the story develops. By the way, Chris, we never mentioned anything about what this job might pay. Don't you think that might be appropriate?"

"The way I see it, money is not our hero's major concern," Chris responded. "He's financially at ease and has no doubt that he will be properly compensated for his efforts."

"Fine," Jonathan laughed. "Keep in touch."

Chris cut the connection, inserted Melissa Etheridge's 'Never Enough' CD into the player and, as 'Ain't it Heavy' started blaring through the speakers, headed home to Sandy.

Chapter 8 - Tuesday, January 21, 1997

"Ladies and Gentlemen," Charles Peterson called out to open the brief meeting. "I would like you all to meet Mr. Chris Barry. As some of you may be aware, Chris was the driving force behind CSS until its recent acquisition by CompuCorp and is also somewhat of a computer genius. He is currently in semi-pre-retirement and has graciously offered to help us document our computer systems following our recent tragic loss of George. I trust that you will all appreciate his presence and join me in welcoming him in his temporary stay with us. I also hope that you will do what you can to help him in any way possible."

A murmur of "Hi's", "Welcome's" and nods of greeting emanated from around the boardroom table.

Seated to the immediate left of Charles Peterson at the head of the table, Chris rose to his feet to address the group.

"I'd like to thank Mr. Peterson for his overly flattering introduction. I know very little about your business but I do know computers to some extent and will do my best to put together the appropriate documentation so that your next M.I.S. guy can get a head start. I know that I'm gonna need everybody's help on this and just want to thank you in advance for any support you can give me."

He paused to clear his throat then went on.

"Now, everybody knows who I am but I have no idea who you all are. If nobody has any objections, I'd ask everyone to introduce themselves. With a little luck, I'll remember a couple of names and look less like an idiot in the days ahead."

Following a round of chuckles and smiles, the man seated to Peterson's right gave Chris a friendly wink as he spoke.

"Wayne MacKinnon, Director of Operations. Pleased to meet you, Chris."

"Hey, Wayne," Chris replied.

"Greg Pierce," the small bespectacled man next to Wayne announced, almost uneasily. "Director of Finance."

"Nice to meet you, Greg," Chris responded, smiling at the obvious accountant.

One by one, the remaining individuals seated around the table introduced themselves while Chris studied each face, making mental notes to remember who was who.

"Well, I thank everybody for their words of welcome and I promise not to be shy if I need a hand," said Chris once the process was over. "Now, if you'll excuse me, I'll go sit quietly somewhere and try my best to figure out what the hell I've got to do."

Chapter 9 - Wednesday, January 22, 1997

By the end of his second day at Quality Imports, Chris had managed to accumulate enough information about the firm as well as its employees to create a starting ground for his investigation.

The company had been founded by Charles Peterson ten years earlier, who still owned eighty percent of it. His directors of operations, finance and sales each had a five percent share. The remaining five percent now belonged to the estate of the late George Robinson, but would be purchased back by the company, this according to regulations in the charter stipulating that shareholders had to be employed by the firm.

Charles had indicated that, as per past practice, this block of shares would eventually be awarded to George's successor, once merit had been established. He believed that managers tried harder when they owned a piece of the pie and, the success his business had known thus far appeared to fully support his theory.

Prior to becoming his own boss, Charles Peterson had been the purchasing manager for Roosevelt's, a major textile importer and distributor. At the age of forty, he had been informed that, due to rightsizing, one of the popular management trends of the time, his services were no longer required.

On the following day, Charles had rented a small office and with the help of his already established contacts overseas, had founded Quality Imports and gone into direct competition with his previous employer. Within six months, he had turned his one man operation into a flourishing business with two dozen employees, including the best sales people from his former employer. A year later, he had acquired Roosevelt's, which was by then on the verge of bankruptcy, having lost a number of key accounts.

As things progressed, Peterson's firm had moved into the importation of other products ranging from mini-blinds and athletic shoes produced in Asia to coffee beans from Columbia. Today, over three hundred were employed.

The business itself was quite simple. Having established a reputation for low prices and a rather wide (and ever growing) distribution base, Quality Imports was able to purchase an impressive variety of products at high volume, hence, low cost. Prices were marked up only enough to cover expenses and provide a modest profit on a per item basis. However, what the company lost in margin was more than made up for in volume.

A quick look into the firm's financial records indicated that it was healthy, generating a profit of approximately $5 million per year. Of this, 10% was distributed to its handful of shareholders as dividends, proportionate to their percentage of ownership in the company while another 20% was distributed to the firm's remaining population in the form of profit sharing bonuses. The end result was an efficiently run organization where everyone pitched in to improve service and reduce operating costs.

When comparing the company's financial records to its banking and investment records, Chris could not identify anything that seemed out of the ordinary. There did not appear to be any large excesses of cash or other assets in comparison to the company books. A first glance clearly indicated that the

48

firm was on the up and up and not involved in any illegal or fraudulent activity.

But just because the cops had been advised to look into Quality Imports didn't mean that the company itself was involved in any wrongdoing. It could very well be some of the players within the organization who required investigation. To this effect, Chris had easily extracted the names, addresses, social insurance numbers and bank account information from the company's payroll system. With this information in hand, he would be able to run some checks on each individual to see if anyone might be involved in any underhanded activities.

He glanced at his watch and was surprised to see that it was nearly 7:00. He tossed a couple of reports, which he hoped to look at after dinner, into his briefcase and headed towards the side door where he was parked.

As he walked past the glass-walled reception hall at the front of the building, he noticed an Econoline, followed by a Jaguar, turn into the parking lot. He stopped and watched as both vehicles headed towards the west side of the building and rounded the corner, out of sight.

Intrigued, Chris hurried to the side door, on the east side, and quietly exited. He was pleased to note that the parking area on this side of the building, which was reserved for visitors, was not illuminated. As he unlocked the Pathfinder, he casually scanned the area but saw no-one. Satisfied that his presence had not been detected, he started the engine and quickly left the grounds, heading east, away from the side of the building where the two vehicles had gone.

A quarter mile further, he turned right and at the next intersection, turned right again. By driving another quarter mile, in the opposite direction now, he found himself in front of a warehouse located immediately behind the

Quality Imports facility. He pulled into the shelter of a recessed shipping dock and, leaving the truck, rapidly headed towards the rear of the warehouse on foot.

At the back of the lot, some seventy-five feet behind the building, were several piles of skids which would serve well as an observation point. Thankful for the early evening darkness, he crept across the open space to the welcome cover of the skids, confident that he had not been seen.

A hundred feet away were the Jaguar and Econoline, parked by an open door of the Quality Imports' shipping area. One man, unknown to Chris, appeared to be keeping watch, concentrating his attention towards the front of the building, apparently not expecting any intruders from behind.

A muffled shout was heard from inside and the watchman moved to the elevated shipping dock where another man had appeared with four wooden cases on a hand truck. One by one, the obviously heavy cases were transferred into the Econoline. As soon as the fourth case was loaded, both men climbed into the van and drove off.

As Chris watched on, two other figures suddenly appeared in the still open doorway and these, he did recognize; Wayne and Greg, Directors of Operations and Finance. Greg appeared nervous, glancing furtively about, twitching and pacing back and forth. He muttered something, which Wayne responded to with a laugh and a shake of the head.

The latter reached inside and the lights went out as the huge door began to descend. As Wayne jumped off the four foot dock, Greg gingerly climbed down the short steel ladder affixed to its side, drawing another head shake and laughter from his colleague. They hurried to the Jag and climbed in, Wayne in the driver's seat, and, seconds later, sped off into the night.

Chris checked the time; 7:08. From start to finish, their little visit had only taken eight minutes. He wondered what could be important enough to bring four men here on a Wednesday night in January for such a short stay? Maybe the variety of products imported by the company was wider than he had been told.

He was starting to believe that he would truly enjoy this job. He returned to the Pathfinder and headed home to Sandy.

Chapter 10 - Thursday, January 23, 1997

"I'm gonna have to find out what's in those boxes," Chris informed his lovely wife as they chatted over breakfast.

"It's guns or drugs," Sandy confidently guessed. "What else could it be?"

"Stolen art, bacterial weapons, I don't know," Chris responded, shrugging his shoulders. "But you're probably right; guns or drugs."

"So these guys are probably dangerous."

It was a statement, not a question.

"I'll be real surprised if they're not," admitted Chris, knowing where this was going. "Yes, my love. I'll be careful."

"Is there anything I can help you with?" Sandy offered, ignoring his last comment.

"Actually, I think there is," Chris replied. "Peterson is paying me to document his systems so I'm gonna have to start working on that if I want to stick around. Which means I won't have time to do some other stuff. I copied some information off the payroll system to run a check on everybody working there. What I'm looking for is anything that would indicate someone living much beyond their means."

"Like a shipping clerk with a yacht and condo in Maui?" Sandy playfully suggested.

"Yeah, anything like that," Chris replied with a grin. "Think you can handle it, kiddo? There's about three hundred people to look into."

She knew exactly how to go about digging into other people's lives through the computer. She had seen Chris do it hundreds of times during his Vigilante days.

"Piece of cake, Mr. Barry," she replied confidently, leaning over to kiss him. "I was trained by the best."

* * * *

"That new guy, Barry, he makes me nervous," stated Greg.

He was seated in Wayne's comfortable office along with Wayne and Bryan Downey, Director of Sales.

"Ah, Jesus, Greg," retorted Wayne in disgust. "Your goddamn grandmother makes you nervous."

"I just don't like having some unknown person digging around here, that's all." Greg shot back. "I have this strange aversion to spending many years in prison."

"What *do* we know about this guy?" Bryan quietly enquired, as usual the mediator between these two extreme personalities.

"He was EVP at CSS," Wayne arrogantly replied. "He's a computer genius, semi-retired, filthy rich. He just wants to do a little contract work as a bridge between working constantly and doing nothing at all. Christ, I can understand the guy. He's what, maybe thirty-five? He's just trying to slowly withdraw from the workforce. I see no reason to worry about him."

"Is there any danger of his finding anything out?" Bryan pressed.

"No fucking way," answered Wayne, annoyed. "He's here to document our systems. He's not gonna *find* anything on our systems."

He stopped suddenly and stared at Greg, his eyes narrowing. "I trust you weren't stupid enough to set up our records here, were you?"

"Of course not," Greg shot back, indignantly. "It's all on my PC at home. Sometimes I access the files from here through Eazy-Com but nothing is recorded here."

"So then, what's to worry?" challenged Wayne. "All he can find out is that Quality Imports is a well run, profitable business. All the transactions are kosher, all the suppliers real. Everything is under control, guys."

"Hey, I'm comfortable," Bryan retorted defensively. "I'm just making sure that Greg isn't worrying about something concrete."

He turned towards the fidgeting accountant. "Relax, Greg. I'm sure Barry won't be a problem."

"Alright, if you say so," Greg doubtfully replied, forever uneasy. "I just don't want any more screw-ups."

* * * *

It had been a while since Chris had done any systems analysis and he was quite enjoying himself. Maybe he would seriously consider taking on a couple of free-lance contracts per year as a hobby.

Peterson had settled him in the late George Robinson's office, where he was currently busy reading lines of code and drawing a flowchart.

"So, how's it going so far?" questioned a voice from the doorway.

"Good, Charlie. Good," he replied to Peterson. "Maybe your man wasn't keen on documenting what he did but he was a damn good programmer. Real clean work, no patches or plugs; just straightforward and logical."

"I'm happy to hear that," said Peterson. "I just wanted to see how you were doing. Let me know if you need anything."

"Sure thing. I do have question for you while you're here. Do you operate on multiple shifts?"

"Nope. Day shift only, eight to five," Peterson responded. "Volume's not high enough yet for extra shifts but we'll get there."

"Any special orders sometimes that someone might come back to look after in the evening?" Chris persisted.

"Not really. Maybe a little overtime on busy days but normally, when we lock up we do so for the night. Why?"

"Well I noticed that some of the inventory control programmes had some cut-off times worked into them, probably to ensure proper stock levels," Chris explained. "I haven't finished going through them yet so maybe some other programme lines compensate. I'm presuming that further into the programme, I'll run into some code that sets off the running of back-up jobs. In any case, I was just concerned that entries made after a cut-off time might not record in the system."

As he had hoped, Chris could see that Peterson had no idea what he was talking about. In all fairness, Charlie *had* admitted that he knew squat about computers.

"All I know," repeated Peterson with a look of confusion. "Is that we've only got one shift; eight to five. That's it."

With that, he turned and walked away.

Chris held back a smile as he watched the departing man and murmured under his breath, "And that's all I wanted to know. Thanks, Charlie."

Chapter 11 - Friday, January 24, 1997

With cup in one hand and computer print-out in the other, Chris returned from the coffee machine, reading as he went along.

"Good morning, Mr. Barry," a familiar voice called out as he walked by the reception hall.

He stopped and turned towards the voice, breaking into a warm smile as he identified the speaker.

"Lieutenant McCall," he exclaimed with exaggerated formality, tucking the printout under one arm to extend a hand.

Chris and Dave McCall had worked closely together several months earlier on the Vigilante case and had grown quite fond of each other. It was Chris's guidance which had led Dave and his team from the Special Homicide Task Force to the late Carl Denver, the supposed Vigilante.

"*Captain* McCall to you, sir," Dave McCall barked in insult as they shook hands.

"Well, excuse me," Chris jokingly retorted. "How the hell am I supposed to know when you don't keep in touch. So you made captain. Good for you. When are you gonna head the force?"

"Next year," Dave replied with a grin, "One step at a time. So, how have you been?"

"Fine, great," answered Chris, gesturing towards a hallway. "Come on in to my office for a few minutes."

"So, what the hell are you doing here?" queried Dave once they had settled into Chris's temporary quarters. "I thought the papers said you had retired?"

"Well, I realized that it would be best to ease out of the labour force," Chris explained. "So I decided to do a little contract work here and give this place a hand until they find a new M.I.S. Manager."

"Yeah, well as you may have guessed, I'm here to talk about the last M.I.S. Manager," Dave sombrely said. "You're aware of what happened?"

"Uh-huh," Chris nodded. "The top cop looking into this? Is this a major case?"

"Nah. It's probably just a mugging gone bad," Dave responded. "I just have less and less time to get out on the street so, every once in a while, I pick a routine investigation and handle it myself. Just to keep my blood running. Did you know the guy?"

"Nope," replied Chris. "I didn't even know this company until about a week ago when an acquaintance mentioned it. I saw an opportunity for Quality and I to help each other to our mutual benefit. I made a proposition and Charlie Peterson agreed to it so, here I am."

"Well, good for you," said Dave as he glanced at his watch; 8:57. "I'm gonna get out of your hair cuz I have an appointment with Peterson at nine. Listen, give me a call. You and I have to get together real soon. We've got a lot of catching up to do and, from what I read in the papers, now you can really afford to buy me dinner."

"You shouldn't believe everything you read in the papers," responded Chris with a smirk. "I'm just a poor soul trying to get by."

"My heart bleeds for you," laughed Dave as he left the office.

* * * *

Dave's meeting with Charles Peterson had proved to be a waste of time and effort and, although this was what he had been expecting, he had to follow up on all possible leads. Unfortunately, murder investigating was a business of trial, error and luck, not at all an exact science.

Peterson had described the late George Robinson as a quiet, friendly individual who, though not socially active, got along well with everybody. Originally from Calgary, he had moved to Montreal about ten years ago and had joined Quality Imports less than a week later. His sole passion was computers and they occupied most of his waking hours.

He had no immediate family, being an only child and having lost his parents in an automobile accident five years earlier. Peterson, who truly did not believe that George had any enemies, attributed his employee's untimely demise to simply being at the wrong place at the wrong time.

To date, nothing had indicated anything different to Dave and he was inclined to agree. Unfortunately, in this day and age, there were lots of nasty people out there.

As he drove across the Des Prairies River on highway 15, with George Robinson's useless death on his mind, his thoughts strayed to the Vigilante. Maybe they should have left him alone. He *had* been supplying a valuable service to the population at large, making the world a safer place for its honest citizens.

Although Dave recognized that the man had been a criminal, he couldn't help but feel some respect for him and for what he had undertaken.

59

Dave himself had often had to fight off the urge to pull out his gun and blow some punk away. Knowing that they were back on the street before one even finished the paperwork was, at the very least, goddamn frustrating. But the law was the law and they had to play by the rules.

He allowed his mind to wander again as he drove and Chris Barry popped into mind. He was surprised, yet happy to have seen Chris. Shortly after the solving of the Vigilante case, he had been promoted and the size of his task force had been increased. Unfortunately, murder was a growing business.

At about the same time, CSS had been put up for sale so both he and Chris had ended up with very busy fall schedules and little time for social activities. He would make a point of getting together with Chris in the near future however, as he truly enjoyed the man's company. He chuckled suddenly as he realized that what had created occasions for them to see each other thus far were murders. He'd have to warn Chris to stay away from such events lest he want to be considered a suspect.

* * * *

"So like I was saying, Mr. Johnson, we realized that we had too much space for nothing. That's when we built this wall to cut off our warehouse from this side of the building and sectioned off this side into smaller storage areas. Most of our clients are local businesses who need occasional space for temporary overstocks."

"Well, this will do just fine," said Chris, nodding approvingly as he peered out towards the rear of the building through the windows of the office above the storage area. "You see, the mini-warehouses I saw were just too small. My parents have been living overseas for a number of years and now, my father has retired and they're moving back here. While their house is being built, they're gonna fulfil a lifelong dream and go for a trip around the world for a few months. In the meantime, they're shipping all their stuff here, including a car, and I have to put it somewhere until the house is ready. Plus, there's some furniture they bought, so on and so forth. Bottom line is, I need a place to stick it all and this would be perfect."

"It's available if you want it," replied Tony Bradley, owner of the building located directly behind Quality Imports. "You can take one closer to the front if you want. Like you saw, they're all pretty much the same."

"No, I'd like this one," insisted Chris. "I might use the office occasionally and this one has windows. I like to see outside."

"Your call," Tony shrugged indifferently. "They all cost the same; a thousand a month."

"That's fine. Three months should be all I need. Is cash O.K.?"

"Sure," agreed Tony with a huge grin. "Cash is great."

"Excellent," said Chris, pulling out his wallet and starting to count. "There you go, Mr. Bradley; three thousand. I'll let you know if I need it longer."

"Hey, you're welcome to stay as long as you want, Mr. Johnson," exclaimed Tony, admiring the wad of bills he clutched tightly in his fist. "And if you need anything else, don't be shy. I aim to please."

Chapter 12 - Saturday, January 25, 1997

Chris put away his breakfast dishes in the dishwasher, being careful not to make any noise which might wake Sandy. She had worked late on some research for him the previous evening and deserved her sleep.

He poured himself another cup of coffee and headed downstairs to his workshop. He was nearly finished working on the equipment he needed and planned to go install it at his newly rented warehouse later that day.

After starting up 'Cracked Rear View', the first CD by 'Hootie and the Blowfish', he resumed his work on the modified video cam he had clamped to his work bench. Fifteen minutes later, the few remaining connections were complete and the transmitter was in place, set to the proper frequency. All that remained to be done was the testing.

He picked up a stopwatch, started it and placed it in front of the camera lens. After turning off the CD player, he headed for the garage, choosing the Lexus 400SC for his little ride. The roads were dry and at 6:45 a.m. on a Saturday, he figured he could speed a bit with little risk of getting pulled over.

Within minutes he was on the 40 heading west and then north on the 640. Twenty minutes later, he was approaching the Quality Imports building, heading west again, this time on the 440. He pulled out his cell phone, called a number stored in memory and gazed down at the Sony Watchman on the seat beside him.

Following a few seconds of static, the tiny picture cleared and he could see the stopwatch ticking away back at home. Twenty-four minutes, thirty-seven seconds. He punched a second memory number on the phone and the screen went blank.

At Chomedey Boulevard, he crossed over the 440 and headed back east. As he approached Quality Imports, from the west this time, he looked at his watch. Five minutes had gone by since his last transmission. He recalled the first memory number on the phone and the miniature T.V. screen came back to life. Thirty minutes, three seconds. He smiled with satisfaction as he called yet a third number from memory, this one aimed at turning off his little network altogether.

At 7:39, he rolled the Lexus back into its spot in the garage and hurried to his work shop. He pressed the rewind button on the video cam and listened to the whirring sound of the tape. It stopped after fifteen seconds or so. Smiling with satisfaction, he pressed the play button. As the image of the stopwatch appeared on the camera's small view-screen, he leaned forward to verify its time recorded on the videotape. Twenty-four minutes, forty-three seconds. He watched the recording for the next five minutes until it ended; at thirty minutes, five seconds. He smiled again and headed upstairs for another cup of coffee and the morning paper.

* * * *

"Good morning, sir," yawned Sandy as she shuffled into the dining room where Chris sat reading the paper.

63

"Well, it's about time," teased Chris, tossing the paper aside. "I've been up for hours, I'll have you know."

"Yeah, so?" Sandy replied as she leaned down to hug him from behind. "That's cuz while *I* was doing *your* work, *you* were sleeping."

"Oh yeah? Well you better have something good for me," retorted Chris with mock sternness, heading for the kitchen to get her some coffee.

"If you're not satisfied, boss," she called out with a sly smile, "You can hold off on those sexual favours I crave for."

"And risk a complaint to Employment Standards," he snorted, returning to the dining room. "Not a chance, lady."

"What a relief," Sandy sighed as he handed her a cup of coffee. "Thanks. Now sit down and I'll give you my report."

"Great. What did you find?"

"Three of the top boys at Quality seem to be doing extremely well financially," she proudly started, referring to a computer printout she had brought down with her. "Wayne, the operations guy, has been buying real estate for a couple of years now. Mostly apartment blocks, commercial buildings, that kind of thing. Places that generate income. He owns well over twenty million in rental properties, in addition to several extremely expensive homes which are either occupied by members of his family or used for recreation. He currently has no mortgages or loans outstanding."

"Maybe he's just a sound financial planner," kidded Chris. "What else?"

"Greg, your Director of Finance, lives pretty conservatively. One house, nice, based on the price, but not extravagant; his real money's into investments; stocks, bonds, mutual funds. He's also worth a lot more than what he gets paid at Quality; many millions more."

"Who's the third?" asked Chris, not surprised about the first two.

"Bryan Downey," replied Sandy, "Director of Sales."

"I've only met him once, briefly," admitted Chris, "On my first day when Peterson introduced me to everybody."

Sandy continued. "He seems to be a flashy one; a number of properties, all apparently for his personal use. One is his main residence in Laval-sur-le-Lac. He also has condos in Vancouver, Palm Beach and Santa Barbara and villas in Oahu, Phuket and Maracaibo. He seems to like big toys because he currently owns nine expensive cars, three boats including a sixty foot yacht, not to mention a helicopter."

"Jesus, I've got to get myself a full-time job at this place," exclaimed Chris with a playful air. "Anybody else?"

"The supervisor of the receiving department earns $36,000 a year and is living in a quarter million dollar home and driving a sixty thousand dollar car. The two lead hands in receiving both have comfortable properties, fully paid for. One also has a second residence in St-Sauveur while the other has an eighty thousand dollar yacht parked at the Oka Marina. These guys earn $26,000 a year so I guess they must do a lot of overtime."

"Anybody else seem shady?" Chris enquired.

"Not from what I could dig up. If anyone else is involved, they're not getting paid much or they're doing a much better job at hiding the extra cash. You've got addresses, makes of cars, names of boats, everything in here."

She slid the computer report across the table to him.

"Well, I must say Ms Taylor, you've done some excellent work," commended Chris, standing and reaching for his wife. "I don't know how I'll ever repay you."

"Think a little," Sandy replied as she removed her oversized sweatshirt, revealing her firm naked body underneath. "I'm sure something will come up."

* * * *

After a memorable morning with Sandy, Chris had reluctantly switched his mind back to the task at hand and headed to his warehouse behind Quality Imports. Before leaving, he had made a few last minute adjustments to some of the hardware he would be using and he was anxious for a final test.

Although Tony Bradley had assured him that nobody went into the rented warehouses, Chris had changed the locks on both the shipping dock and walk-in doors and had also installed door alarms for good measure. He did not want anybody nosing around.

His observation camera was now in place in the second floor office window from where one had an excellent view of the shipping doors at Quality Imports where he had seen Wayne and company the previous Wednesday. It was time to see if the whole thing worked.

He pulled his cell phone from his pocket and retrieved a number from memory. The 'record' light on the video cam came on but the usual whirring of the tape could not be heard; so far, so good. He punched another number on the phone and listened to the ringing while waiting for a reply.

"Hi, gorgeous," answered Sandy back at home.

"Hey there. So, you got your breath back?" he enquired teasingly, referring to their morning together.

"Just barely," she laughed. "But I should be in shape for another round when you get back."

"Whoa, sweetheart. Gimme a break," he groaned. "Don't forget, I'm a retiree."

"O.K., I'll wait til tonight," she conceded with a chuckle. "By the way, the VCR started just before you called. What I can see is the back of a warehouse with an occasional car driving by on the highway in front. I presume that's what you wanted?"

"Yes. Great," Chris replied. "I'm just about done here. I'll see you in a little while."

"Be careful," Sandy responded. "Bye."

He had been bothered with having the tape in the video cam. First of all, it limited the recording time to eight hours which would have meant having to show up at the warehouse much more frequently to change the tape, therefore increasing the risk of being seen. Secondly, if somebody did get into this place, they could easily grab a possibly valuable tape.

To overcome these problems, he had installed a receiver on the VCR at home, hoping that the image would transmit properly via the cell phone network. It worked. Basically, his system was simple. He had set a switch and transmitter in the video cam which was activated by phone. One frequency started the camera and transmitted the signal to the receiver installed in the VCR. Another frequency also sent the image to the screen of his Sony Watchman. A third simply turned off the whole network. Ingenious. He could now track the questionable activities of some of his new co-workers in relative safety.

He'd look into the possibility of setting up another camera inside the Quality warehouse but recognized that that would be risky. He wouldn't want anybody to spot it and he certainly wasn't interested in having anybody walk in on him during the installation. He would have to think about that one carefully.

Pleased with his accomplishments thus far, he left his warehouse, locking the door securely behind him and arming the alarm system with a remote control he produced from his jacket pocket. He quickly crossed the paved yard and moved onto the property of his temporary employer, towards the second leg of his journey.

Satisfied that he was alone after having walked the perimeter of the building, he entered by his usual side door, pausing only long enough to enter his security code into the alarm control pad. As he started his tour of the premises, he turned on his cell phone and pressed the appropriate keys, activating his surveillance camera. His Watchman came to life, displaying the empty yard by the shipping doors.

Within fifteen minutes, he had completed his visit of the front section of the building, having concentrated his attention on the offices of Wayne, Greg and Bryan. He moved on to the warehouse area, waiting a moment for his eyes to adjust to the low illumination. Not quite certain of what he was looking for, he started to wander slowly through the aisles, keeping his eyes open for anything of interest.

As the minutes went by, he became engrossed in his search, poking into boxes and crates, amazed by the variety of merchandise stored in the place. He sauntered into another aisle where he noticed a number of familiar looking wooden cases. Maybe he'd get to find out what had been in the ones he had seen on Wednesday night.

Examining the first crate, he noted that it was securely nailed shut. He went back to a wrapping station he had passed two aisles earlier and returned with a small crowbar. As he got to work on the case, the warehouse was suddenly flooded with light.

"Holy shit," Chris muttered under his breath, pulling the Watchman from his jacket pocket and staring at the screen while he fumbled for his cell phone.

A black Maxima was parked below the shipping dock. He pressed the appropriate keys and the screen went dark. He'd have to be less stupid in the future. For now though, he had a problem to solve and he had no idea where his problem was or if he was alone. He couldn't hear any conversation which he hoped meant he was dealing with one person only.

He concentrated for a moment, thinking back to Sandy's computer report which he had scanned before leaving; Black Maxima. One of the receiving lead hands, Rick something. That might come in handy if he came face to face with the guy.

He considered his options and decided that, if at all possible, he preferred to just get the hell out for now. It was too early in the game to get caught snooping around.

He started backing up slowly towards the side aisle, listening for any sound which might indicate the visitor's whereabouts. He felt something against the back of his leg and realized, too late, what it was. The crowbar clattered to the concrete floor, its metallic jangle, without a doubt, the loudest noise that Chris had ever heard.

Footsteps rapidly approached along the central aisle and Chris started towards them, crowbar in hand.

"Who's there?" he demanded in a loud, firm voice as he rounded the corner.

Rick, some fifteen feet away, stopped in his tracks as this somewhat familiar looking man appeared before him wielding a crowbar.

"Who the fuck are you?" Rick nervously asked, keeping his distance as he pointed the small pistol he held at Chris.

"Chris Barry. I'm working on the computers until they find a new guy. You're Rick, right?" Chris asked, relaxing his stance a bit as he lowered the crowbar.

"Yeah, that's me," Rick replied, also relaxing slightly. 'What are you doing here?"

"My wife and I got into a fight," Chris responded, grinning sheepishly. "I figured I'd come in and work a little while she blows off some steam."

Rick snickered and seemed more at ease. "What were you snooping around back here for?"

"I was in my office and I saw a car go by. When I didn't see it come back, I came to make sure everything was O.K."

Rick, visibly relaxed now, took a few steps towards Chris. 'I'm sorry, Mr. Barry. I just wasn't expecting anybody here. I thought somebody had broken in."

"Seems like you would have done O.K. even if that had been the case," suggested Chris, gesturing towards the gun.

"Oh, shit. Sorry, Mr. Barry," Rick exclaimed, tucking the small weapon into the back of his pants. "We've had some problems here before. One of our guys got beat up pretty bad. That ain't gonna happen to me."

"Good for you, Rick. Good for you," said Chris encouragingly. "Listen, if everything's under control, I'll get out of your hair and get back to work. It was nice to meet you."

"Sure, Mr. Barry, nice to meet you too."

The two men shook hands and headed their separate ways, Chris towards the front offices and Rick to the back of the warehouse.

Chris hurried to the side door by which he had come in, entered his security code and exited. He moved quickly towards the rear along the east side of the building, activating his camera as he went. The Maxima was still visible on the screen but Rick was nowhere in sight. He rounded the corner, scanning the area to make sure no chance witnesses were present but the place was deserted. As he approached the next corner, he slowed his pace and looked at his screen, smiling as he saw himself.

He waited for a moment and saw Rick appear with cardboard box in his hands, heading for the Maxima as the trunk popped open. As Rick leaned forward to load the carton into the car, Chris moved in swiftly and silently behind him, the crowbar raised high. He swung it down forcefully, delivering a solid blow to the back of Rick's skull. He quickly flipped the unconscious man into the open trunk, pausing only to retrieve his victim's car keys and gun before closing the lid.

"Sorry, Rick," Chris murmured softly. "I didn't want you to tell your friends I was here and, I was curious to find out what you guys have in those boxes. Let me get you somewhere more comfortable so you can sleep. You and I can talk later."

Chapter 13 - Sunday, January 26, 1997

Chris strolled up to the door of his rented warehouse, disarming the alarm with the remote control as he approached. He had parked a couple of blocks away, as he had done the previous day, to avoid having his vehicle spotted. He unlocked the door, wondering how his guest was this morning. He hoped Rick had slept well.

He had been angry at himself yesterday for his carelessness and had sworn that nothing similar would happen again. But in retrospect, he was happy with how things had turned out and how easy it had been.

He had driven the Maxima around the block and brought it to his warehouse. The pull-out ramps installed within the loading dock had made stashing the car child's play. He had pulled Rick's still unconscious form out of the trunk and, with the help of a roll of filament packing tape and a support post in one corner, had ensured that his visitor would be no trouble.

Rick was awake but still in the position Chris had left him, seated on the floor and securely taped to the post behind him. He glared at Chris as the latter approached to check if his wrists and ankles were still properly bound.

'Good morning, Rick," Chris cheerfully greeted. "Did you sleep well? Silly me; how can I expect you to answer me with that tape on your mouth?"

He bent over and, with a swift jerk, ripped off the tape, causing Rick some obvious discomfort.

"You goddamn motherfucker," Rick bellowed, trying to rub his painful face on his shoulder.

"I'm standing here, completely free and mobile," Chris stated calmly, "While you're sitting there, totally helpless and vulnerable, taped to a pole. I suggest you be careful how you talk to me, Rick. Understand?"

"Fuck you," screamed Rick. "You don't know who you're dealing with, asshole. You're a dead man."

"Rick, Rick, Rick. You just don't seem to realize who's got the big end of the stick here," Chris muttered, shaking his head. "How can you threaten me? You're not being logical. Think, man, think."

"They're gonna kill you," Rick insisted. "You're gonna regret the day you decided to fuck with them."

"Who's gonna kill me, Rick?" enquired Chris, obviously not shaken by his prisoner's threats.

"Fuck you, you son of a bitch," Rick shot back. "You'll find out soon enough. I ain't stupid enough to give you a lead."

"Are you talking about Wayne and Greg?" Chris suggested. "Or do you mean Bryan? Oh, I know. Maybe you're talking about Bob, your boss, or Matt, that other little shit that works with you."

Rick's face paled noticeably as the various names were mentioned, drawing a smile from Chris. Barring the verifications that Sandy had made, Chris had nothing specific linking these individuals to any criminal activity. Any one of their comfortable financial positions might have been explained by an inheritance, a lottery or a rich parent. Rick's initial reaction however, seemed to confirm the involvement of the named parties.

"So which one should I be worried about, Rick?" Chris continued. "Are they all killers or just some of them? But maybe they're not into murder. Maybe that's your job. Maybe you're the guy who shot George."

Rick's body stiffened and the fear was apparent on his face.

"Bullshit. I didn't do it," he blurted out. "And there's no way you could prove that I did."

"I'd have to disagree with you on that," Chris smoothly replied. "I've got your gun and a boxful of coke. The cops have a dead body. Put everything together and it fits. You're in for life."

"The cops'll see it ain't my gun that did it," Rick argued, doing his best to seem confident.

"Oh come on, Rick," Chris snorted in disgust. "How stupid are you? Do you think the cops give a fuck if it's the right gun? They'll know you were into some kind of shit. So what, maybe you didn't kill George. Somebody's gotta pay. They take your gun and shoot a few rounds into a side of beef. Then they pull out the slugs and replace the ones they had taken from George's body. Bingo. Dead body, your gun, your slugs, your murder."

"Th-they can't do that," Rick cried out. "That's, that's wrong."

"That's life, Ricky-boy," Chris responded with a laugh. "There's got to be a guilty party."

"Well, I don't buy it," Rick spat out defiantly, another attempt at courage. "The cops can't pin George's murder on me and you're still in really deep shit. That's all I got to say."

Chris sighed, shaking his head as he pulled up a chair. He sat down and stared at his guest for a moment before speaking.

"I want you to listen very carefully to what I have to say because it's important. There are only two people who know where you are right now; you and me. That's it. There's also nobody else who knows or even suspects that I had anything to do with your disappearance. So your threats on my life don't impress me. In fact, they're starting to really annoy me."

He paused for a few seconds, continuing to stare at the younger man with cold, unblinking eyes. He believed he now had Rick's full attention.

"Now, you've mentioned a few times that I don't know who I'm dealing with. Well, I'll let you in on a little secret, my friend. *You* don't know who *you're* dealing with. You said you didn't kill George and Rick, I believe you. I don't think you ever killed anybody because you wouldn't have the balls to do it. Now me, on the other hand, I've killed people; many times. Sometimes I beat them to death with a baseball bat. Other times, I slashed their throats. Once, I had this guy suspended by his wrists and used him for target practice. I must have shot him fifty times with his own guns. Oh, and another time, there was this pusher who sold crack and smack to little kids. I tied him up and injected him with the biggest goddamn overdose you ever saw. So, you see, I *have* killed before. I know how to do it and I do it well. I could easily do it again."

Another short pause allowed his words to clearly sink in.

"Do you know what kind of people I killed, Rick? I'll tell you. My victims were criminals; the nasty kind; murderers, rapists, wife-beaters, pushers, that kind of thing. Do you realize Rick, that you and your friends fit that category? You guys are just the kind of garbage that I used to eliminate as a hobby. That's who you're dealing with, Rick."

The hard look previously on the young man's face had been replaced by one of petrified fear. He obviously believed what his captor had said and began to visibly tremble, despite his sturdy restraints.

"W-w-what are you gonna do with me?" he stammered in a quivering voice.

"Who killed George, Rick?" Chris asked, his tone quiet, serious, deadly.

"They're gonna kill me, man," Rick pleaded.

"Believe me, my young friend," said Chris, almost gently. "That is not your primary concern right now. Who killed George?"

"Jesus, man, can't you give me a break?" cried Rick, now sobbing.

Chris responded with a cold, hard stare, saying nothing.

"He's gonna fucking kill me, man," Rick screamed. "And it'll be on your fucking head. Wayne did it. Wayne shot George cuz he found some coke."

"Who was there when Wayne shot George, Rick?" continued Chris, unmoved by his prisoner's emotions.

"Me, Greg and Matt," Rick muttered between sobs.

"Who dumped the body?"

"Me and Matt got him into the trunk of his car. Then I drove it into town and Matt followed me. I parked and took off with Matt. But we were just following orders from Wayne. You gotta believe me."

"I believe you so far, Rick. You're doing good. Keep it up. Now tell me about this little business you gentlemen have going. How does it work?"

"I don't know much," Rick admitted.

The answers were flowing freely now.

"Me and Matt, we're like gofers, errand boys. We receive the stuff, do deliveries, that kind of thing. Wayne pays us five thousand a month, cash."

"Who's supplying the stuff? Where's it coming from?" enquired Chris, happy with Rick's cooperation. It made the job so much neater.

"I don't know who. It comes from Asia, Columbia, places like that," answered Rick, hopeful that his helpful attitude would play in his favour. "Bob, our supervisor, tells us when a shipment comes in. Matt and I look after those pallets and put the merchandise in the overstock area. Then, in the evening, we all come back and take the stuff out and put the merchandise back into the proper locations."

"Wait a minute," interrupted Chris. "Explain that to me in a bit more detail. What merchandise?"

"The stuff comes in with other stuff we import. Like, say we get some coffee. Well, there'll be some coke packed into the middle of the crates. Mini-blinds come in from Asia and have heroin stashed in the bottom rail of each blind. That kinda thing."

"Impressive," commented Chris, nodding thoughtfully. "You guys must have somebody at customs working for you?"

"I guess," replied Rick, actually starting to relax. "I know that for those shipments, we don't use the same broker that we use for the regular stuff we import."

"Who do you use for these special shipments?"

"Rapid Forwarders. Our contact there is Andy. I've spoken to him a few times. I don't know his last name."

"Anything else of interest that you might want to tell me?" asked Chris, convinced that the kid had played straight. He surely wasn't the mastermind behind this operation.

"No. Nothing that I can really think of," Rick replied emphatically. "Like I said, I don't know much. It's not like I'm running this thing. I'm just an employee."

"Does Peterson have anything to do with this?"

"Shit man, no way," Rick responded, actually breaking into a smile. "Old man Peterson thinks grass is hard drugs. I've seen him fire guys a couple of times on the rumour that they smoked dope. He'd freak if he ever found out."

"Well, I think you've given me all the information you could. You see, Rick? Wasn't it easier this way, with you cooperating?"

"Yeah, except that now I'm a dead man," Rick replied sullenly. "I'm gonna have to disappear. And if Wayne ever gets a hold of me, he'll kill me."

"Don't worry about Wayne, Rick," Chris said with a soothing smile. "He'll never get a hold of you. I'll make sure of that. I'm gonna help you disappear so well, he'll never be able to get to you."

"Can I keep the drugs I took?" asked Rick hopefully. "That would at least give me some cash to start off."

"Yeah, Rick. O.K. You can take some of the coke. Anyhow, I promise that you won't have to worry about any future financial problems."

Chapter 14 - Monday, January 27, 1997

"Come on in, Bob," invited Wayne from where he sat behind the large desk in his office at Quality Imports.

Also present were Greg Pierce and Bryan Downey.

"Close the door behind you, Bob. Have a seat."

The silence which ensued quickly made Bob, Quality Imports' receiving supervisor, uncomfortable.

"Can somebody tell me what's going on?" he asked after several seconds, not having the faintest idea why they wanted to see him in the first place.

"Where the fuck is Rick, Bob?" demanded Wayne in an accusing tone.

"How the hell should I know?" Bob retorted, suddenly feeling persecuted.

"Well, he's your goddamn employee and he's not fucking here," Wayne shot back angrily. "I figured you'd have some goddamn idea of what the fuck your employees are doing."

"What the hell is going on?" asked Bob, glaring at the three other men.

"What the hell is going on?" mimicked Wayne in a surly tone. "I'll tell you what the hell is going on. That little bastard was supposed to pick up four keys of coke here and deliver it on Saturday. He never showed up for the delivery and our client is not happy. Now, we can't find the little prick anywhere and the coke is gone. That shit's as pure as you can get, Bob. Once cut, it's worth over a million on the street."

"Rick wouldn't do something like that," Bob defensively argued, having been the one who brought Rick into the business. "He knows what crossing us could mean."

"He knows what crossing us could mean," repeated Wayne sarcastically. "A million bucks can encourage a twenty-five year old punk to do a lot of stupid things, asshole."

"He's not at home?" Bob queried, scrambling for a logical explanation.

"I tried to call him a few times Saturday night when I found out that he hadn't showed up for the delivery," Bryan dejectedly responded. "We called again yesterday and Wayne went over to his place. His car wasn't there and neither was he."

"Maybe he had a wild weekend with one of his bimbos," Bob hopefully suggested.

"He has four kilos of snow, Bob," growled Wayne in frustration. "Why would he pick up the dope and then decide not to deliver and party with a broad instead?"

"Have any of you considered the fact that maybe he got arrested?" asked a sweating Greg Pierce. "He might be spilling everything he knows to the cops right now."

Silence filled the room as everyone realized that Greg's suggestion was a definite possibility.

"W-we would have heard something on the news," said Bryan unconvincingly.

"Yeah, right," snorted Wayne in disgust. "Whenever the cops bust a punk with a million dollars of blow, they automatically call the reporters to make sure anybody else involved gets tipped off nice and proper. You ain't too bright sometimes, Bryan."

"Hey, fuck you, Wayne," Bryan retorted, pouncing from his chair towards the other man. "I ain't the one letting high school drop-outs run around with four kilos of coke."

"Gentlemen, please," cried Greg in exasperation. 'I don't think this is the time to argue about your levels of stupidity. We've got to figure out what happened to Rick. In the meantime, we should assume the worst and presume he was arrested, which means, let's shake our ass and get whatever fucking shit we have here, out of here."

Greg's use of profanity was practically non-existent. When Greg started swearing, he was serious.

"Greg's right," stated Wayne, his tone more controlled. "Bob, you go have a serious talk with Matt. See if he knows anything. And I do mean *anything*. And go over to Rick's place again. Get inside and check it out. Greg, what's our current inventory?"

"The four keys was all the coke we had left. The next delivery is Wednesday, twenty-five kilos. We have half a dozen keys of heroin but Bryan has three of those sold. Another shipment will be in on Friday; ten kilos."

"O.K." said Wayne, thinking furiously. "Bryan, call our guy with the Aces of Death. Tell him we'll get him three keys of horse for the same price we had agreed on for the four keys of coke. That's a great deal for him and it'll clean out our inventory here. I'd like you to deliver it personally cuz he was really pissed off with Rick's no-show on Saturday. If we get in with these guys, we can really start moving some shit. Talk to him about the stuff we have

81

coming in this week. I want it out of here as soon as it gets in. We're gonna have to play real careful until we find out what happened to Rick."

* * * *

Wayne paced back and forth in his spacious office, consumed with frustration, anger and, especially, fear. They had to find Rick and until they did, keeping the business going could be extremely dangerous.

The timing for this could not have been worse. Although they had done very well since they had started importing drugs a few years ago, they were now on the verge of making some really big money. The Aces of Death had a strong hold on the drug trade throughout Quebec and had solid ties with two major biker gangs in Ontario which controlled the market there. Combined, these two provinces held close to sixty percent of the country's total population of close to 30 million, which was not a negligible customer base. Wayne's contacts in Asia and South America had informed him that production was now running to perfection so they could supply whatever volume he required. As it was, the Aces of Death organization was currently looking for one supplier with the capacity to cover their entire needs. Everything had seemed perfect.

A light tapping at the door broke into Wayne's thoughts.

"Excuse me, Wayne," said Chris Barry. "You got a minute?"

"Sure, Chris, sure," Wayne forced a smile, gesturing towards a couch in the corner. "Have a seat. We haven't really had a chance to chat much since you joined us. I've been pretty busy. Sorry."

"No need to apologize," Chris responded reassuringly. "I'm no stranger to heavy workloads and busy schedules."

"What can I do for you?" asked Wayne, settling into an armchair across from Chris.

"Well, actually," replied Chris, looking a little troubled. "I wanted to tell you something that might be of interest to you. Maybe it's nothing but I thought you should know."

"Sure. What's up?" asked Wayne, feigning interest.

"Saturday afternoon, my wife and I were out shopping and on our way home, we happened to drive by here so I stopped to show her the place."

Wayne leaned forward in his chair, his interest in what was being said suddenly much more genuine.

Chris continued. "We came inside and I was showing Sandy my office when I saw a black Maxima drive by towards the back of the building. We continued the tour and just as we walked into the warehouse, the lights came on. I went to the main aisle and called out and one of the guys from receiving, Rick, he said his name was, came walking up the aisle towards us. When he recognized me, he relaxed a little but he seemed nervous the whole time we chatted. He asked me what we were doing here and I explained and introduced my wife. I asked him what he was doing there and he told me that a customer needed a rush order and you had asked him to get it. His story was plausible but, like I said, he really seemed nervous and that left me wondering. When he saw that we were turning back towards the offices he seemed relieved and hurried back towards the shipping area. My wife and I left the building and I walked over to the west side to look down towards the rear. I could see the Maxima parked by the shipping dock and they were putting a box in the trunk."

"They?" Wayne interrupted, sounding concerned. "Rick wasn't alone?"

83

"Well, I thought he was when I saw him inside but there were two guys with him at the car. I didn't want them to see me and think I was spying on them so I headed back to the other side where I was parked. As I was getting ready to leave, I saw the Maxima pull out onto the road and take off. They seemed to be in a hurry, which made it seem even stranger."

"I see," said Wayne with a stern look on his face. "Something's definitely wrong here, Chris, because I never called Rick about any special order. I wonder what they took?"

"I couldn't tell you," Chris ruefully replied. "I was pretty far so all I can say is that it was a cardboard box, not too big."

"Hey, don't worry about," Wayne reassured him. "We'll check the inventory to try to find out what's missing. This might explain why he didn't show up this morning."

"Oh really?" Chris questioned. "Do you have anything valuable enough that somebody would abandon a job for?"

"Well, we do import some electronic components that could be worth a couple of bucks," Wayne explained, obviously angry. "If he found a market for them and has been taking stuff for a while, it might be worthwhile."

"Wouldn't somebody have noticed an inventory short?" enquired Chris.

"Yeah, I guess. Eventually," admitted Wayne. "But some of this stuff is only used by a few customers who aren't very good at forecasting. They don't order often but when they do, it's in massive quantities and it's needed for yesterday. So we stock up heavy and it sits in our warehouse for a few months until suddenly, it all goes at the same time. Until that order is placed, we wouldn't know that anything was missing unless we did a physical count and we only do those once a year, in October."

Chris nodded in understanding. "So Rick might have been stocking up for a couple of months by now."

"It's possible," replied Wayne in frustration, "The little bastard. I better not get my hands on him."

"Well, anyways, that's what I wanted to tell you," Chris said as he stood. "Let me know if I can help you with anything. I'd be interested in knowing what happened to Rick when you find him."

"Sure thing, Chris," Wayne agreed.

He stood and extended a hand.

"Thanks for the info. I'm sure that what you saw on Saturday will help. By the way; those two guys you saw with Rick. What did they look like? Did you recognize them as some of our other employees?"

"No, I'm pretty sure of that," Chris replied decisively. "They looked kinda rough if you ask me. You know, like bikers maybe, that kind of thing. There again, I was pretty far so I wouldn't be able to give a great description. But they seemed to be wearing blue jeans and leather jackets and both had long hair. One had a beard."

"O.K., good. That might be helpful. One last thing; did you talk to Charlie Peterson about this?"

"Nah," Chris replied with a wink and a smile. "You know how those top guys are. They blow everything out of proportion and make mountains out of nothing. You're the operations guy; you're the one I came to."

"You're a good man, Chris," said Wayne, winking back. "And a good judge of character. You've got Peterson down pat. Thanks again. I'll keep you posted."

He waited until Chris had closed the door on his way out before picking up the phone. He punched in a few numbers and waited impatiently, swearing under his breath until someone picked up.

"Bob. Rick was here on Saturday with two biker types. Barry happened to be here, showing the place to his missus and he saw them loading a carton into the Maxima. Find that little cocksucker and bring him to me. I will personally show him what happens to little bastards who try to rip us off."

* * * *

"I still don't think Rick would have tried to steal the coke," Matt stated determinedly as he and Bob drove through the streets of St-Eustache to Rick's home. "And if he did, we sure as hell ain't gonna find him sitting around his place."

"Listen, Matt," replied Bob in an annoyed tone. "He picked up the four keys on Saturday and disappeared. He was with two guys when he went to the warehouse. He knows better than to bring somebody to the warehouse. He ripped us off. I know we're not gonna find him sitting at home but Wayne said to check, so we check."

They drove the few remaining minutes in silence. As they turned the corner onto Rick's street, they were surprised to see the black Maxima parked in the driveway of their co-worker's residence.

"Well I'll be a sonovabitch," Bob muttered under his breath. "The asshole **is** home."

He parked a few houses away and they proceeded warily on foot, examining Rick's house as they approached but noticing no apparent activity.

"You got your gun?" asked Bob in a low voice.

"Y-yeah," replied Matt in a quivering voice.

He found the drug running exciting and profitable but the recent murder, and now this, was somewhat less appealing.

"Well, don't use it unless you have to," warned Bob. "I don't want the neighbours calling the cops about gunshots."

They reached Rick's residence and slowly crept up the driveway, still looking for any signs of movement inside or out, but saw none. As they moved on to the front door, they noticed the weekend's accumulation of flyers and local newspapers sticking out of the mailbox. Maybe Rick wasn't there after all.

After glancing around for possible witnesses, Bob grasped the door handle, slowly depressed the latch and gently pushed inward. Offering no resistance, the door opened; it was unlocked. He looked nervously at Matt, uncertain of what to do next or what to expect inside. The house might be empty or this could be an ambush. They stepped quietly into the vestibule and closed the door behind them.

"Now what?" Matt mouthed soundlessly.

Bob pulled a revolver from his jacket pocket while thinking of an action plan. Finally, deciding that indicating their presence might be interpreted as a wish to avoid confrontation, he called out softly.

"Hello. Is anybody home? Rick, are you here? It's Bob and Matt. We were worried about you."

They listened for any sounds of movement, anything which might indicate somebody else's presence, but heard nothing.

Bob motioned Matt forward, barely whispering, "Slowly."

They crept silently ahead, searching frantically for any sign of activity. As they moved past the wall which separated the living room from the vestibule, Bob turned his head and gasped. Sprawled on a couch was Rick's dead body, a syringe still protruding from his arm.

"Oh, fuck, man," mumbled Matt. "I'm gonna be sick."

True to his word, he made a serious mess on the thick pile carpet.

"Get a hold of yourself," hissed Bob. "Come on. Let's check the rest of the house. There may still be someone here."

They continued their painstakingly slow search, which was interrupted on two occasions by Matt's additional bouts of nausea, but found the house to be void of other occupants. Their search complete, they went into the kitchen, both badly in need of a drink. After draining a first beer, Bob picked up the phone to call Wayne.

"Yeah, it's me," he grimly announced as he popped open his second beer. "We found him. The asshole overdosed. He's still got a needle stuck in his arm. Yeah, at his place. Car's in the driveway, the front door was unlocked. Nope, we didn't find it yet. We'll look a bit more to see if it's around or if there's a bundle of cash stashed somewhere but I ain't promising anything. Yeah, I figured that's what you'd want us to do. We'll get rid of him. I don't know where but I'll make sure nobody finds him for a while. Don't expect us back today."

He hung up the phone and looked at Matt who was sitting at the kitchen table, still in a daze.

"Finish your beer and get your act together, boy," Bob said with a smirk. "We've got ourselves a body to make disappear."

* * * *

Chris lay sprawled comfortably on a couch in the den watching the T.V. screen with an amused smile. He heard the shower stop upstairs and a moment later, smelled her light soapy perfume as she entered the room behind him.

"Don't try anything you might regret," he playfully warned. "I know you're there."

"Well, with the line of work you've chosen, Mister," she replied sternly. "You sure as hell better."

She leaned over him from behind the couch and with his assistance, slowly crawled over its back, all while delivering a rather passionate kiss.

"What are you watching? A cop show?" she asked as she snuggled up against him, clad only in a large towel.

"Something like that," he responded, his attention now equally divided between the screen and her inviting body beneath her scanty attire. "It's my surveillance tape from this morning. Their morning started with a 'Where the hell is Rick?' discussion, followed by my bullshit story to Wayne. You see those two? That's Bob, the receiving supervisor on the left. The other guy is Matt, the second lead hand. They were on their way to find Rick."

"How do you know all this?" asked Sandy, knowing that her husband would have an intelligent explanation.

"While I visited Quality on Saturday, I happened to plant a few mikes in Wayne's, Greg's and Bryan's offices. Secondly, since the phone system is linked to the mainframe, it was pretty easy to set up a recording and monitoring system this morning. Let me zap this a bit. O.K. Here we go. There's one of Bryan's toys, as you put it; a Mercedes 42D SEL. That's him getting out of the car. Now, you see that box he's carrying? That, my dear, is

6.6 pounds of high quality heroin which he's going to deliver to the Aces of Death."

"My God," Sandy cried in alarm. "Chris, do you really think you should mess with these guys? I mean, Jonathan did tell you that you were on your own."

"No, no, no," Chris soothingly disagreed. "All Jonathan said was that if I got caught doing something illegal, he couldn't vouch for me. If I need some help, I can call him and he'll send another consultant."

"So call him," Sandy said with a pleading undertone.

"I will, if and when I need help. Right now, I'm just setting things up. Anyways, you know I like to work alone."

She gave him a scolding stare which initiated a quick comeback.

"But as soon as I need help," he promised with a grin, "I'll call Jonathan."

"You're such an asshole sometimes," she stated with a pout, bringing her knees under her chin and exposing more than her thighs in the process.

"Yes I am," admitted Chris, moving in on the exposure. "But I hope you'll always love me anyways."

"Always," she moaned as she leaned back and shifted her thoughts to the matter at hand.

Chapter 15 - Tuesday, January 28, 1997

Clad in fish-net stockings, leather jacket, mini-skirt and bra-less under her tight sweater, the sexy young blonde strutted up to the main desk of the St-Eustache police station.

Gazing at her in awe as she approached, Sergeant Robert Savard wondered if he should ask for her hand in marriage, simply invite her over for sex, arrest her for prostitution or offer assistance. After seriously considering his second option, he opted for the last.

"How can I help you, miss?" he gallantly enquired, staring at this vision of loveliness.

"My boyfriend's missing," she replied a matter-of-factly.

"I see," said Sergeant Savard, making a valiant effort to concentrate on the serious nature of the business at hand. "Did you and your boyfriend have a fight, Miss, uh?"

"Rousseau," answered the bombshell. "Louise Rousseau. And no, Ricky and I didn't have a fight. Ricky and I get along really great."

'I'm sure you do. I know I would,' thought Savard before asking, "What makes you think he's missing, Miss Rousseau?"

"Well, Ricky and I saw each other Friday night and he said he'd call me on Saturday, but he didn't," she whined. "He does that sometimes but usually, he calls the next day to explain how he got tied up with some business. But Sunday he didn't call and yesterday either."

"Maybe he's just been really busy, Miss Rousseau," Savard replied sympathetically, starting to realize that God might have sacrificed this one's brains for her heavenly looks.

"No," Blondie disagreed. "I called him at work yesterday and again today but they told me he's not there. I went over to his house but he's not there either, but his car is. Ricky loves his car. He wouldn't go anywhere without it and if he did, he'd at least put it in the garage."

"When *did* you last see Ricky, Miss Rousseau," asked Savard, uncertain if she was just wacky or if her concerns were truly founded.

"Friday," she repeated. "When I went to his house, I checked around and all his clothes and stuff are still there. He just disappeared and I'm worried."

"O.K." Savard gave in, figuring her statements at least deserved some looking into. "What's your boyfriend's name?"

"Ricky, Richard Beauchamp."

"His address and phone number?"

"327, Landry. 472-1289."

"Age?"

"I'm not sure," she giggled. "About twenty-five, I guess."

"Can you describe him?"

"Well, he's pretty cute," she replied with a shy smile. "Blonde hair, usually tied in a ponytail. Well built but slim. He's about five, nine and weighs, I guess, around a hundred sixty pounds."

"O.K. We'll see what we can do," said Savard, writing a case number in the appropriate box on a witness information card. "Could you complete this for me? If we find anything, or need more information, we'll be able to get in touch with you."

"Sure," she responded, flashing a killer smile at the young, handsome cop. "Don't hesitate to call."

'At least, if this turns into nothing,' thought Savard, 'I'll have her name and phone number.'

She completed the card and, after another heart-stopping smile, left with a hip swaying stride that caused heads to turn and kept Savard hypnotized until she was out of sight.

Once she had gone, he returned to reality and the routine of entering the data he had just collected into the National Police Information Network.

* * * *

Greg finished re-reading his entry and, satisfied with what he had written, saved the text on his home PC and logged off from Eazy-Com. He had neglected his journal for the past few days which was something he did not like doing.

He had started writing it four years ago, the very day that Wayne had first proposed the smuggling of drugs along with the company's legal shipments. At first, Greg had thought Wayne was kidding, but his colleague had quickly demonstrated how serious he really was. Contacts had already been established with drug suppliers as well as with some of the firm's regular suppliers. Customs brokers and officers interested in some additional cash had been identified and approached. The network had already been established. All that had been required was a little investment of time and cash and their new business was born.

Greg had never imagined being involved in any kind of illegal activity. He had difficulty jaywalking without troubling his conscience. However, the financial possibilities of Wayne's proposition had been overwhelming. No legal investment, no matter how lucrative, could generate an equivalent return and, Greg loved money. That was what had drawn him to the field of finance in the first place. He had accepted to go into business with Wayne and had started his secret journal.

His journal was an insurance policy for him and it was therefore important that he keep it constantly up to date. It contained a complete description of all their activities, down to the smallest detail; dates, names, quantities, amounts; it was all in there. If he ever got busted, he would be certain that everyone went down with him. In fact, Greg sincerely believed that the information in his journal could win him complete immunity and a new identity. Should something ever happen to him, such as an untimely demise, a letter addressed to his lawyer would be found in his safety deposit box. It contained instructions and appropriate passwords allowing access to his journal.

"Yes," Greg thought with determination as he watched the main menu reappear on the computer screen. "If anything ever goes wrong, many people are going to pay."

* * * *

From the comfort of his office, Chris watched his computer screen go blank for a fraction of a second, followed by the reappearance of the main menu. He pressed a few keys and the image generated by Greg Pierce's PC

94

disappeared from the monitor, to be replaced by the lines of code he had been working on earlier.

"Works like a charm," he breathed to himself, proud of his programming capabilities.

All the PCs within the building were linked to the mainframe, thus allowing them to double as terminals. Thanks to this network, tapping into the PCs of any of his suspects was made relatively easy. With a little bit of programming, he had established a monitoring system which recorded the activity taking place on their computers at any given time. As an additional gadget, he had foreseen a flashing icon, which he could turn on or off at whim, which informed him of any such activity. He could then link on to the PC in question, his screen becoming a double of the other computer's monitor.

Greg had just been unknowingly kind enough to create the opportunity for Chris to test the system and, it worked. Chris, with growing interest and amusement, had read Greg's words as they were being produced. The man kept a diary. And Chris could only guess that it would provide some extremely interesting reading.

He would have to visit Greg's home computer shortly and he was certain that doing so would prove to be a very easy task. After all, not only did he have the address, he also had the passwords.

* * * *

Bryan strolled into Greg's office to find Wayne, Bob and, of course, Greg, waiting for him.

"Sorry I'm late," he apologized as he closed the door. "You know how it is in sales; work, work, work, work."

"Yeah, yeah, sit down," grunted Wayne, not the biggest fan of Bryan's bubbly, salesman nature. "This shouldn't take very long. I just want us to get into the habit of having a quick daily chat for the next little while. I don't like it when things don't go smoothly and I want us to keep each other informed of what's going on. O.K.?"

All heads nodded in agreement as he continued.

"First thing I want to talk about is the Aces of Death. How much do you trust these guys, Bryan?"

"As much as you can trust a bunch of fucking bikers," Bryan chortled. "Listen. They're pushers, pimps and murderers. But they're also the major channel of distribution for our dope, especially for the volume we'd like to move. We've done a couple of deals with them so far and they haven't tried to screw us. I think they're comfortable that we can deliver what we said we could and they love the quality of the shit so far. Plus, they're completely removed from the importing of the stuff which they definitely like. So, to answer your question, I trust them enough to keep on doing business with them and to become filthy rich in the process."

"All right," replied Wayne, unable to disagree with his colleague's logic. "Let's just be real careful with these bastards. Rick was supposed to deliver to our friend 'Diamond Jimmy' on Saturday. He showed up here with two guys that looked like bikers and the next thing we knew, Ricky was dead and we had lost a bunch of snow. I don't want that to happen again."

"Yeah, we'll keep our eyes open," Bryan agreed before turning his attention to Bob. "While we're on the subject of Rick; what's the status with our dead little friend?"

"It's all been taken care of. Matt and I drove up north, way up, to dump the body. We took him into the woods and buried him. Believe me, it was no easy task. The ground's goddamn frozen this time of year."

"Well, a little sweat won't kill you," chided Bryan. "It's about time you did some of the dirty work."

"What the fuck is that supposed to mean?" Bob fumed, rising from his seat.

"Oh, Jesus Christ. Sit down," ordered Bryan, not the least bit swayed by the other man's aggressive reaction. "I'm just saying, Bob, that we've all done our share of crap; Wayne, Greg, Rick, me, even Matt. We've carried enough shit with us to do life if we'd got caught. When did you ever make a delivery, Bob? Never. You got your cushy job inside, away from any danger."

"It was never planned that way, Bryan," said Greg quietly in Bob's defence. "I'm sure Bob will do more if we need him to."

"Well I hope so," Bryan muttered. "We've gotta share the risk is all I'm saying."

"And I'm doing my share," Bob stated defiantly, staring coldly at Bryan for a moment before going on. "Now, about Matt; we're gonna have to keep an eye on him. He's pretty fucked up since we found Rick yesterday. I think the events of the last few weeks might be too much for him to handle."

"Well, he better *learn* to handle them!" growled Wayne. "We're paying that little fuck lots of bucks to handle *anything* that happens. Keep a close eye on him and if he shows any signs of cracking, let me know. We don't have time for this kind of crap. Anything else?"

"One last thing," Greg spoke up, "About Saturday when Rick was here. Don't you find it strange that Chris Barry just happened to be here to see him? I'm still not comfortable with having him around."

"Peterson hired him to document the systems," Wayne responded in a slow, strained voice. "That's what the man is doing. I've seen some of the stuff he's put together so far and frankly, he's damn good. For the first time in years, I understand how some of our systems work. Stop worrying, Greg. Barry's just a nice guy doing his job. Leave it alone."

* * * *

In his office, Chris removed the tiny earpiece and returned it to his jacket pocket.

'Wayne, my friend,' he thought with a smile. 'I thank you for your kind words and your vote of confidence.'

He accessed Eazy-Com and linked up with his computer at home. He had to learn more about the Aces of Death and one of their members, Diamond Jimmy. He was certain that he could find some useful information in the databases from his recent 'Vigilante' days.

Quickly finding what he was looking for, he read for a few minutes, taking an occasional note when pertinent. Once done, he tapped into Greg Pierce's home computer to pursue his research and, after forty-five minutes, he felt he had gathered enough knowledge to go ahead with his plan.

He pulled his cell phone from his jacket pocket and keyed in a number. It was time to set up a meeting with Diamond Jimmy.

* * * *

Diamond Jimmy sat at his usual table near the rear exit of *'Scandale'*, his favourite strip joint, when he saw the man come in and slowly make his way towards him. He discreetly signalled a fellow gang member at the bar and unobtrusively felt under his jacket for the gun strapped to his side, releasing the safety.

Chris reached his table and asked in a low voice, "You Diamond Jimmy?"

"Who the fuck are you?"

"I'm Bob," Chris answered, sitting down, "A friend of Wayne and Bryan. We spoke this morning."

"I've heard your name before, Bob, but I ain't never seen you," explained Diamond Jimmy. "I like to be sure who I'm talking to."

"I can show you some I.D. if you want," Chris offered, reaching for his wallet.

Diamond Jimmy grinned as he replied, "I.D. ain't worth shit to me. I could show you cards that make me Frank Sinatra. Tell me more about Wayne and Bryan and your organization."

"We don't like talking too much about our organization," Chris responded. "When you talk too much, the wrong people can learn things they shouldn't. We're interested in doing business and you're testing us. One of our delivery boys fucked up last Saturday and you didn't get your blow, four keys. Bryan offered you three keys of smack instead for the same price. We got more coke coming in on Wednesday and a delivery from Asia on Friday. Bryan told you about those too."

He looked calmly at Diamond Jimmy with a slight smile, waiting for the latter to respond. He could tell that he had convinced the man.

"Alright, what do you want from me, Bob?"

"Like I told you this morning, the four keys of snow which didn't happen on Saturday are now available," Chris replied. "Are you interested?"

"You wouldn't be here if I wasn't," Diamond Jimmy answered.

"Good," replied Chris, nodding.

"You got it with you?"

"It's close by."

"Go to the bar and have yourself a drink," said Diamond Jimmy. "When you're finished, go to the can, second stall. You'll find your part of the deal. After, head for the McDonalds one block north from here. In the bathroom, there's a broom closet. Leave the stuff there, just behind the door. Then have a coffee or something and wait until someone asks you for a cigarette. Understand?"

"No problem," agreed Chris, standing. "Nice doing business with you."

"Sit down, Bob," Jimmy ordered. "I ain't done yet."

Chris returned to his seat, gazing calmly at the biker as the latter continued.

"You were real clear that I shouldn't talk to Wayne or Bryan about our little meeting, right?"

"That's what I asked," Chris replied slowly, feeling slightly uncomfortable for the first time.

"That tells me that you're ripping off your buddies to do a little personal business," stated Jimmy with a grin. "Am I right?"

"Yeah, I guess you are," Chris nodded uneasily.

"Don't worry, Bob. I didn't tell your little friends but, silence has a price."

"How much?"

"Twenty percent off what we had agreed to this morning," the biker informed him. "Is that O.K.?"

"I guess I don't have much choice," Chris shrugged as he rose to his feet.

"No you don't," Jimmy smiled. "And Bob, don't try anything stupid. If you do, we're gonna kill you. Have a nice evening."

Chapter 16 - Wednesday, January 29, 1997

As was his usual routine, Nick Sharp started the day with a hot cup of coffee while scanning through the New Activity Report; burglaries, rapes, muggings, drugs, missing persons; same old, same old.

He started to turn a page of the report when something caught his eye; Missing person; Richard Beauchamp, 327 Landry, St-Eustache, long blonde hair, five nine, one hundred sixty pounds. Reported missing by Louise Rousseau, friend and Quality Imports, employer.

"What the fuck is it with that place?" he muttered to himself, wondering if Jonathan had had a chance to look into to it.

He reached for the phone and dialled his covert colleague's number.

"Hey, bud. Howya doing?" he asked, waiting the usual few seconds for Jonathan to activate the scrambler.

"Fine, Nick," replied Addley. "Sorry I haven't had a chance to call recently. I've been busy catching up on some of the work that goes with my official title."

"No problem, Jon," Nick reassured him. "I got a quick question for you. Remember when we talked about Quality Imports a couple of weeks ago? You told me you'd see if you could look into it. I was just curious to know if you had done anything with it."

"As a matter of fact, I did," Jonathan responded. "I've had somebody working on it for a week now but I haven't heard anything from him so far. Why do you ask?"

"The N.A. report has something about a missing person this morning and guess where he works."

"Quality Imports," Jonathan replied, more a statement than a question.

"Yup, Quality Imports. Like I said, I was wondering if you were looking after that place and thought you might be interested in this information."

"Don't worry, Nick. It's in capable hands. I'll get in touch with my guy though, just to see how it's going. Thanks for the call."

* * * *

Chris cruised along the 440, heading west while enjoying the impressive lead guitar from Pink Floyd's 'Comfortably Numb'. As he drove past Industrial Boulevard, his usual exit, the phone rang, interrupting his listening pleasure.

"Chris Barry," he answered.

"Good morning, Chris."

"Well, good morning to you, Jonathan."

"I tried to reach you at the office but was told you weren't in yet."

"Yeah, I have a little errand to run this morning; something to do with our story. To what do I owe this pleasure?"

"Nothing really particular. I just hadn't heard from you recently and was wondering how you were doing."

"I'm doing great, Jonathan. Never better. I've been working on our little project and it's really coming along."

"That's good to hear, Chris. Listen, I heard that somebody where you work was recently reported missing. Do you know anything about that?"

"Absolutely," Chris beamed. "I know everything about it."

"O.K." said Jonathan. "I wanted to make sure you were aware. If you need any help, Chris, don't hesitate to call. I've got other consultants I can recommend and even I have been known to be handy on occasion. I don't want you to get into any trouble."

"Don't worry, boss," Chris replied reassuringly. 'If I need help, you'll be the first one to know."

* * * *

As they had agreed the previous day, Wayne and his cohorts assembled for their daily meeting, this time in Bryan's office. Once all were seated, Wayne started the conversation.

"So, gentlemen, anything new to report?"

"Two things," Greg answered, addressing Bob and Bryan more particularly. "First of all, Wayne and I had a quick discussion yesterday about Rick's disappearance and thought that it would be a wise move to bring it to the attention of the police. We felt that it was something we would have done if we hadn't been aware of what happened to him."

Both Bryan and Bob nodded in agreement.

"Secondly," Greg went on. "The coke we were expecting today came in, as scheduled. We all agreed the other day that we get it the hell out as soon as possible so can everybody stick around tonight so that we can unpack this stuff?"

He was answered with more nods from the others in the room.

"So, Bryan," Wayne spoke up. "You might as well give Diamond Jimmy a shout and see if we can move this through him. Don't sound too pushy. I don't want him to start thinking we got problems or have him looking for discounts. But I do want to get rid of this shit quick."

"Don't worry," Bryan replied confidently. "He said that they were looking for a volume supplier with quality dope. That's what I'll show him we are; nothing more, nothing less."

"Anything else?" asked Wayne, accepting the short silence which ensued as a no. "Good. We'll meet in the warehouse at five-thirty."

* * * *

Dave McCall sat at a table at Le Mirage on St-Martin Boulevard, waiting for Chris. He had had some business to attend to at Laval's central police station earlier that morning and had called Chris to invite him to lunch.

The purpose of their getting together was twofold. For one, Dave enjoyed Chris' company and, barring their brief encounter the previous Friday, they really hadn't had a chance to chat since late September. Secondly, Dave had gone through the new activity report early that morning and had learned of the disappearance of one Richard Beauchamp, employed by Quality Imports. Not one to leave much to coincidence, Dave planned to ask Chris if the latter had noticed anything strange going on at his current place of employment. Chris was a very intelligent and observant man and might have spotted some oddities.

"You invited, ergo, you pay," said the familiar voice from behind him.

"Ah, no wonder the poor get poorer," Dave sighed, rising to greet his friend.

Like school children, they talked up a storm throughout the meal, pausing only to stuff an occasional bite of their jumbo smoked meat sandwiches or fries into their mouths. To hear them, one would have thought that they were two childhood friends who had known each other forever. The fact was the two men had met just a little over six months ago but an immediate chemistry had formed. Their wives had also become close friends after having met towards the end of the summer and they now saw each other on a regular basis.

They finished emptying their over-filled plates and, thoroughly stuffed, leaned back in their chairs to attempt digestion over a cup of coffee.

"There's a little business I was hoping to talk to you about while we're here," said Dave, "Something about Quality Imports."

"Sure. Shoot." Chris responded, curious of what his friend had to say.

"We have a reporting system that generates daily data about all sorts of crimes across the country," started Dave. "All law enforcement agencies are linked to it. I was looking over today's report this morning and there was a mention of a Richard Beauchamp who's gone missing. The guy worked for Quality Imports. Have you heard anything about it?"

"Well, I did hear that the guy hasn't show up for work since Friday," replied Chris, obviously trying to remember what he had heard. "Seems to me, it wasn't the first time this kind of thing happened. I think somebody said that the kid was suspected of having a drug problem. I've only seen him a couple of times myself. He worked out in the warehouse, shipping or receiving. I don't spend much time back there."

"You don't think his disappearing has anything to do with Quality Imports?" Dave queried.

"Why would I think that?" Chris asked, puzzled. "Do you think there's a link between him and that murder?"

"I don't know," Dave admitted. "And it probably is just coincidence. I mean, people skip out on jobs everyday, right? I just noticed the thing on this guy because the name Quality Imports was in the report. Seeing as I had a contact in the place, I thought I'd ask."

"Well, I haven't seen anything weird going on but I can keep my eyes open a bit more if you want," offered Chris. 'You know, go take a walk around every once in a while. Maybe I'll see something."

"Sure, you can do that but don't go out of your way. I don't want you getting yourself into any trouble on my account."

"Don't worry," Chris laughed. "I'm a big boy. I can take care of myself."

* * * *

Bryan had spent most of the day working his real job and making official company sales. By 3:00 p.m. however, he felt that if he wanted to swing a rapid deal with the Aces of Death, he'd better give Diamond Jimmy a call. He keyed in the now familiar number to the biker's phone and waited for a reply which was not long in coming.

"Yeah," Diamond Jimmy gruffly answered.

"Jimmy, Bryan. Howya doing?"

"Getting richer by the pound," replied Jimmy, laughing at his own joke. "What do you got for me?"

"As expected, it snowed today. The forecast was accurate."

"We talking quality?" enquired Jimmy.

"The best, Jimmy. Same as the stuff you should have got last weekend," Bryan replied.

"That I finally got yesterday," Jimmy grinned over the phone. "O.K. We're talking some fine shit."

"W-what do you mean, Jimmy, yesterday?" Bryan asked slowly as his stomach tightened.

"Your man, Bob, cut a quiet deal with me," Jimmy laughed proudly.

"Bob sold you the four keys?" asked Bryan, fighting to control his anger. "Why didn't you call me?"

"Easy, Mister Manager," Jimmy warned. "I don't have to call nobody, understand? Somebody comes to me with a solid proposition, I do business. He gave me a better price than you do. You're lucky I even told you about this."

"Why tell me this now?" questioned Bryan, still fuming.

"Cuz I don't approve of double-crossing little pricks," Jimmy chuckled. "So, you still wanna do a deal?"

"Absolutely, Jimmy," Bryan answered, swallowing his ego, "Same quality, same supplier; twenty-five kilos."

"Alright. Big time," exclaimed Jimmy, apparently impressed with the quantity. "Give me the night to work out the cash and call me in the morning. I think that we're gonna do some fine business together. I won't even ask you for a discount like I did with Bob. Later, Mr. Manager."

Bryan slammed down the phone and stared blankly about, breathing deeply in an effort to control his rage. They had questioned to what extent the Aces of Death could be trusted and, in the meantime, one of their own was screwing them right under their noses.

After a moment, he picked up the phone and punched in Wayne's extension. They would need to have a little chat with their partner, Bob.

* * * *

Chris moved quietly into the warehouse, checking the time as he sauntered amidst the rows of high racking; 5:17.

He walked around casually for a few moments until he was satisfied that he was alone, then headed to the last row of racking and climbed the sixteen feet to the top to settle into his little niche among some boxes. He was certain that they wouldn't find him here. Earlier, he had verified the merchandise within these boxes to make sure it was only what it was supposed to be. He sat back and waited, ready to observe.

* * * *

Wayne pulled the heavy door to the utilities room shut and securely locked it.

"Well, that's it boys," he announced, turning towards the others. "Now all we gotta do is get rid of the crap," he added, looking at Bryan.

"Jimmy said he'd be getting back to me tomorrow," Bryan answered confidently. "We're talking about a bigger load of cash this time but don't worry. This will all be gone in less than twenty-four hours."

"I hope so," Greg pitched in worriedly. "I don't like the way things are going lately. And I still don't trust these bikers. They're probably the ones who did Rick in."

"We don't have any proof of that, Greg," Bryan replied impatiently. "For all we know, Rick overdosed himself and some of his buddies took off with the dope. Whatever happened, I have a gut feeling that it had nothing to do with the Aces of Death."

"Could be," said Greg doubtfully. "But I still think we should be really careful."

"Greg, we're dealing with millions of dollars of smack and coke," Wayne spoke in a condescending tone. 'Of course, we should be really careful. Come on, let's get out of here."

* * * *

As the double garage door glided silently upwards, Bob rolled his black Jeep Grand Cherokee slowly up the driveway and pulled in next to the white Corvette convertible, his summer car.

After cutting the engine, he climbed out of the 4x4 and headed up the five steps leading into the living quarters of his luxurious home, pausing only long enough to step out of his overshoes at the top of the staircase. As he headed towards the kitchen for a beer, he proudly admired his spacious abode, pricelessly decorated by expensive professionals.

"Who says crime doesn't pay," he laughed aloud to the empty home.

He reached the kitchen, tossed his coat on a chair and was on his way to the refrigerator for a beer when the doorbell rang.

"Who the fuck is that," he muttered, changing direction as he glanced at the clock on the stove; 7:47 p.m. "Probably some little punks selling goddamn chocolate bars for school again."

He opened the front door to find Wayne and Bryan standing there.

"Hey guys," he exclaimed in surprise. "Come on in."

He stepped aside to let them enter, closing the door behind them.

"So, what brings you here?" he curiously asked. "Is something wrong?"

"We had something to discuss with you, Bob," replied Wayne, his tone serious. "And we didn't think it was appropriate to talk in front of Greg and Matt. You understand, don't you?"

"Sure, guys. Sure," Bob agreed, unsure of the topic of discussion. "Have a seat. I was just getting myself a beer. You want one?"

"Yeah, Bob. A beer would be nice," Bryan agreed. "Why don't I get them for you. You have yourself a seat."

Their host did not appear to be armed and Bryan certainly did not want to give Bob an opportunity to grab a gun somewhere.

"Yeah, alright," Bob responded hesitantly, growing uneasy. "You know where the fridge is. Go ahead."

He turned to Wayne as Bryan went into the kitchen. "What's going on, boss?"

"Just a little situation we need to talk about, Bob," Wayne replied smoothly. "What do you say we just wait for Bryan?"

Within a moment, Bryan returned with three beers which he passed around to the two others. After each man had opened his bottle and taken a healthy gulp, Wayne resumed the conversation.

"So, Bob? What have you been up to lately?"

"What do you mean?" asked Bob, perplexed. "I don't understand your question."

"Well, then I guess I'll be a little more specific," Wayne became impatient. "What did you do last night?"

"Last night? Nothing special," Bob responded, becoming annoyed and somewhat frightened. "What the fuck is going on, guys?"

"I had a chat with Diamond Jimmy this afternoon," Bryan stepped in. "About the coke we just got. He told me that you delivered four kilos of cocaine to him yesterday."

"What? That's bullshit," exclaimed Bob incredulously, starting to rise.

"Sit down, you asshole," ordered Wayne, drawing a silenced pistol. "Why would Jimmy say that, Bob, if it wasn't true?"

"H-how the fuck should I know?" Bob cried, staring in horror at the handgun pointed at his head. "I don't even know the guy."

"Jimmy was quite specific," Bryan resumed. "He clearly mentioned that it was the dope we fucked up with last weekend and that you called him to cut a deal. Wayne and I were figuring that maybe you had found the coke at Rick's place and decided to make yourself a bit of extra cash? We're thinking you might have even whacked Rick to get your hands on the blow?"

"Wayne, Bryan. Come on," pleaded Bob, sweat starting to glisten on his forehead. "We've been in this together since the beginning. Why would I do something stupid like that for a few hundred thousand? I'm making fine money as it is."

"Well, then. Answer my fucking question. Where were you last night, Bob?" enquired Wayne, his tone soft, but deadly. "Prove to us that you weren't with Jimmy."

"Jesus, Wayne. I was here watching television," Bob cried, now sweating profusely. "This Jimmy asshole is up to something. I never delivered no coke."

"Bryan, why don't you look around a bit," suggested Wayne, apparently unimpressed thus far with Bob's arguments. "See if you find anything interesting. I'll keep an eye on our host here."

* * * *

Still quietly hidden in his elevated hideaway above the warehouse floor, Chris checked the time; 7:45 p.m. The others had been gone for over fifteen minutes now and his Sony Watchman continued to display an empty parking lot.

He climbed down the racking and hurried to his office in the front section of the building to get his briefcase. Returning only minutes later, he quickly headed for the door of the utilities room. Having learned from experience, he kept a close eye on his miniature T.V. screen while he got to work.

As long as the door lock did not give him too much trouble, which he did not believe it would, he'd be on his way to a relaxing evening with Sandy by eight o'clock.

* * * *

"Why don't you get Jimmy over here?" insisted Bob, confused, angry and scared. "At least the cocksucker will have to say it to my face that I brought him the goddamn coke."

"You said it yourself, Bob. Jimmy doesn't know you," Wayne quietly explained. "If that's the case, why the fuck would he make up a story and tell Bryan that some idiot he doesn't even know scammed us and sold him some coke? It just doesn't make any sense, Bob. You tried to screw us and you got caught. It turns out that this biker bastard can be trusted more than one of our own."

"Call the fucker," Bob screamed hysterically. "I didn't do anything. He's goddamned lying. Get the fucking scumbag over here."

"I'm trying to establish a working relationship with the Aces of Death," Wayne replied softly. "If I called Jimmy and even suggested that I doubted what he told us, I don't think he'd appreciate it. I still don't see why he would tell Bryan that you were there if you weren't, Bob. It's that simple."

"Hey, Wayne," Bryan called excitedly as he hurried down the stairs from the second floor. "Look what I found in old Bob's bedroom closet."

He carried a brown leather satchel of a kind familiar to both him and Wayne. To date, the Aces of Death had always delivered payment in such satchels.

"What's this, Bob?" asked Wayne with an unpleasant sneer.

"Th-that's not mine," stammered Bob. "I don't know what that is."

"Open it," Wayne ordered Bryan and the latter complied.

"You just better pray that this ain't full of cash, Bob," Bryan smirked as he pulled open the zipper atop the bag.

After briefly glancing at its contents, he turned the open satchel upside down, dumping the stacks of bills in a pile on the floor.

He turned towards Bob with a knowing grin, pausing a few seconds before speaking. "Somebody's been a very bad boy."

"This is a set-up, guys," Bob pleaded in a quiet voice, tears streaming down his cheeks.

"I just can't see how that can be," replied Wayne, just as quietly.

114

"Good-bye, Bob," he added with finality as he raised the silenced revolver and repeatedly pulled the trigger.

* * * *

As he had hoped and expected, the lock to the utilities room had proved to be of little challenge to Chris and, within no time, his tasks were done for the night.

He left the building and casually strolled to his Pathfinder which he had parked a few blocks away. As he started the engine, he looked at the clock in the dashboard. 7:59 p.m. He smiled as he pulled away from the curb. He had promised Sandy that he'd leave the office by eight.

Chapter 17 - Thursday, January 30, 1997

"Boy, do you guys look like hell," stated Greg, examining Wayne and Bryan as he entered the latter's office.

Glancing around the room, he added, "Where's Bob?"

"Bob's no longer part of the organization, Greg," Bryan grimly informed the accountant. "Bob's the reason that we look like hell."

"What are you talking about?" asked Greg, suddenly feeling queasy. "What's going on?"

"Bob's the one who had the four missing kilos of coke," explained Wayne in a tired voice. "The idiot tried to screw us and went and sold them to Diamond Jimmy. Jimmy mentioned it to Bryan so we paid Bob a visit last night. He denied everything but we found three hundred thousand dollars stashed in his closet. I guess he hadn't had time to go to the bank."

"Where's Bob now?" asked Greg sullenly, although he already had somewhat of a clear idea.

"Up north," answered Bryan. "Sonovabitch kept us up until three this morning. He was right about digging holes in the frozen ground. It ain't easy."

"Does Matt know about this?" Greg questioned, trying to remain calm.

"Not yet," Wayne grunted impatiently. "I'm gonna talk to him later."

"Because they were together when they went to Rick's place," Greg worriedly pointed out.

"You think Matt was in on this?" Wayne asked thoughtfully.

"I'm not saying he was," replied Greg. "I just know that Bob was ice fishing at Saint-Anne-de-la-Perade over the week-end. He dropped off some of his catch at my place on Sunday night when he came back so, I figure the only time he could have gotten hold of the coke is on Monday."

"I'll talk to Matt," said Wayne in an angry, quiet tone. "The little bastard better not have anything to do with this."

"How are we going to explain Bob's disappearance?" Greg nervously questioned.

"Right now, everybody thinks that he's gone on vacation," Wayne explained. "I said he called me last night and told me that he had a sudden opportunity to go to Mexico real cheap with a girlfriend."

"What are you going to say in two weeks' time?" persisted Greg, clearly unhappy with this latest development.

"We'll deal with that when the time comes," Wayne exploded with more than a hint of exasperation. "Maybe the stupid fuck will decide to stay in Mexico."

Bryan broke in, intent on changing the subject.

"In the meantime, we have more urgent matters to attend to. I spoke to Diamond Jimmy earlier and Wayne and I are going to do the deal this morning. This is it, Greg. If you thought we made good money so far, you ain't seen nothing yet. We'll be coming back today with over 1.5 million goddamn dollars. And this will be the first of many."

"Well, that's some good news," Greg listlessly muttered, his expression hardly brightening. "I just hope things start improving. These last few weeks have been getting to me. You guys be careful, O.K.?"

"Don't worry," Wayne confidently responded. "Nothing can go wrong this time. Just wait and see."

* * * *

Wayne and Bryan hurried across the busy, icy downtown street towards 600 de Maisonneuve West, their thirty pound briefcases not making the task any easier. They bustled into the spacious lobby of the upscale office building and boarded an elevator to the fifteenth floor.

"You sure you got the address right?" growled Wayne in his usual antagonizing manner.

"You're a real pain in the ass, you know that?" Bryan shot back. "Yeah, I got the address right. You didn't expect to do this kind of deal in the bathroom at McDonalds, did you?"

Before the argument could progress any further, they reached their floor and the elevator doors opened.

Falling silent, they exited and examined the central lobby in search of their destination. To their left were the offices of some actuarial firm. To their right, the floor-to-ceiling oak doors were tastefully set with a discreet brass name plate:

MURRAY, SOMMERS and GREEN
Attorneys at Law

"Big time," whispered Bryan, impressed as he pulled open the massive door and walked into the expensively furnished reception area.

The lovely young receptionist looked up at them with a smile as she spoke.

"Good morning, Gentlemen. How can I help you?"

"Morning," gruffly answered Wayne. "We have an appointment with Allan Sommers."

She scanned a page of a heavy leather bound volume on her desk and replied, "Mr. MacKinnon and Mr. Downey, I presume?"

"You presume correctly," beamed Bryan, always the charmer with pretty young ladies.

"If you gentlemen would follow me," she invited as she rose. "I'll show you to Mr. Sommers' office. Mr. Sanchez has already arrived."

More than happy to comply, they followed her down a hallway to the door of a corner office. She knocked lightly and waited obediently for an acknowledgement before opening the heavy door.

"Misters MacKinnon and Downey are here to see you, sir," she announced before stepping aside to grant them entrance.

Wayne and Bryan entered the huge office, impressed by its obviously expensive decor and furnishings.

"Thanks, Nancy. That will be all," Sommers dismissed her from behind his mammoth desk. "Gentlemen. Come on in. I believe you have already met Mr. Sanchez."

On this occasion, Diamond Jimmy Sanchez hardly looked like the head of the Aces of Death which he was. Wearing an Armani suit, his long hair pulled back tightly in a ponytail, he could easily have been mistaken for a lawyer or at least, a very rich client. But, of course, he was in fact, the latter.

"Nice suit, Jimmy," said Wayne with a grin.

Smiling back, Jimmy replied, "Thanks, Mr. Manager. Maybe one day, you can buy yourself one just as nice. Let's make some business."

"Gentlemen," Sommers spoke on cue. "There's coffee and anything you might like to drink at the bar. The attaché case on the table is for you. If you want to make yourselves comfortable and verify Mr. Sanchez's part of the deal, he and I will go into the next room and make sure your merchandise is satisfactory."

With that, he picked up the two briefcases his guests had arrived with and followed Diamond Jimmy into an adjoining conference room, closing the door behind him.

"This is great," Bryan gushed once they were alone. "This is how to do business."

"It sure beats the piss smelling bathrooms that Jimmy usually deals in," admitted Wayne, giving in to the excitement. "Yep, Bryan, this is how it'll be from now on. Let's get us some coffee and get to work. We got ourselves a shit-load of money to count."

Twenty minutes after Diamond Jimmy and Sommers had left the office, the latter opened the door and addressed Wayne and Bryan.

"Gentlemen, could you join us for a moment," he announced sombrely. "We appear to have a slight problem."

"You're fucking right, we got a problem," Diamond Jimmy could be heard bellowing from the other room. "We got a big fucking goddamn problem."

The two men followed Sommers into the adjoining conference room where the twenty-five bags of coke were separated into two distinct piles on the table. Diamond Jimmy sat in one of the huge leather chairs in one corner of the room, his feet propped up on the table. There was no doubting the rage on his face.

"What's going on?" challenged Wayne. "What problem do we have?"

"You fuckers trying to screw me," hissed Jimmy. "That's the problem."

"Those," Sommers said quietly, pointing to the smaller of the two piles, "Are powdered sugar."

"What the fuck," Bryan exclaimed. "Bullshit. We tested every bag last night. What is this, Jimmy?"

"What the fuck is what?" snarled Jimmy, "You saying that I'm trying to rip you off, you fat motherfucker? I'll throw you out the fucking window."

"Calm down, Jimmy," soothed Wayne. "Nobody's accusing you of anything. Just let us see the bags. I want to know if they've been tampered with."

"What the fuck are you talking about, man?" accused Jimmy, a vicious look in his eyes. "I thought your network was perfect."

"It is, Jimmy," Wayne hastily assured. "This is just a minor internal problem that you're already aware of and we've already started to address it."

"You better finish addressing it," Jimmy shot back. "If this kind of shit happens again, you're a dead man."

Angered by the threat, Wayne retorted, "Don't worry about our end of the business. And from now on, you want to deal with us, you talk to me or Bryan. Nobody else. This kind of crap like you did with Bob is what creates problems like this."

"You want me to deal with you exclusive? That's fine," Jimmy snorted. "But don't make it like your problems are my fault. Keep your guys and your shit under control. Your guy called me Tuesday morning and told me he had the dope. I said fine and we set up a meet. I ain't guilty. I'm just a businessman."

"What time did he call you on Tuesday?" asked Bryan, suddenly curious.

"Who the fuck cares," the biker arrogantly replied, "Around eleven-thirty, maybe. Why?"

Wayne shot a furtive glance at Bryan. They had been with Bob and Greg most of Tuesday morning and all four had gone to lunch together afterwards. Maybe Bob had made the delivery but he certainly hadn't made the call.

"Just trying to see how the bastard set it up," Bryan replied with a shrug.

For a moment, he considered questioning further but figured Diamond Jimmy was pissed off enough as it was. Any more digging would serve to confirm the doubts the biker already had about them and would vastly increase the risk of losing the Aces of Death business altogether.

Apparently thinking along the same lines, Wayne changed the subject.

"Anyways, right now we've gotta get this fake coke thing sorted out. And believe me, this won't happen again."

* * * *

Chris concentrated his efforts that morning on his documentation work for Quality Imports.

As far as the drug ring went, he believed that he already had enough information to bring the whole thing down. Greg's complete diary to date had been copied on disks which were now safely stored in a safety deposit box.

These were accompanied by tapes of pertinent conversations which had taken place since he'd installed his surveillance equipment as well as records of telephone and Eazy-Com communications.

He had contacted Jonathan and was meeting him for lunch to discuss the progress of their story. In Chris' opinion, the next step was to deliver this information to the police and let them 'legally' dismantle the drug importing network and he was certain that Jonathan would agree.

"Bother you for a minute?" Charles Peterson asked, entering Chris' office.

"Sure, boss. What's up?"

"The local Chamber of Commerce is holding one of those 'exchange business cards' cocktails tonight, from five to seven. My staff and I always attend and I was wondering if you wanted to join us; might give you the opportunity to build some contacts for some future freelance work."

"Sure. Why not," agreed Chris, wanting to make his effort to be part of the team. "Where's this thing taking place?"

"At the Sheraton, just up the road."

"No problem, Charlie. I'll be there."

* * * *

Wayne and Bryan rode in silence on the way back from their meeting with Diamond Jimmy. He had agreed to buy the coke they had, eighteen kilos, the seven bags of sugar being their problem. Upon their departure, Jimmy had re-emphasized the fact that they had one last chance. Any further screw-ups would cost them dearly.

"Maybe it wasn't Bob," Bryan stated softly, breaking the silence. "Maybe we killed him for nothing."

"Yeah, well it's a little late to figure that out," snarled Wayne, fixing his gaze on the traffic ahead.

"But if it wasn't Bob, who could it be?" worried Bryan. "Matt?"

"I don't think Matt's got the balls or the brains to try to screw with us," Wayne replied. "Anyways, why would he rip off the coke and leave the money at Bob's? Where's the gain?"

"Maybe he and Bob were in this together," suggested Bryan. "Maybe Matt called Jimmy while Bob was with us. That would give Bob an alibi if we caught on to anything afterwards."

"I don't know," Wayne responded doubtfully. "Granted, they're not the smartest people I've ever met but it's a damn flimsy plan. I mean, if either one delivered the coke to Jimmy, they'd have to realize that he could identify them afterwards. Logically, if you ripped off some dope, wouldn't you go sell it to somebody other than your regular customer? I would. It doesn't make sense, Bryan. I'll have a chat with Matt, but something's wrong. I think Bob was set up and, so were we in the process. Somebody wanted us to kill Bob."

"Who?" asked Bryan, the anxiety in his voice apparent.

"Probably the same person who switched the coke for sugar," Wayne replied in a deadly tone. "This fuck is trying to play with our heads. I don't know who it is, but when I find out, I'm gonna rip his heart out."

* * * *

Chris walked into Moe's and spotted Jonathan seated at a small table in the bar.

"Hey, bud," he chanted as he slid into chair across from Addley.

"Greetings to you, sir," replied Jonathan, extending a hand over the table. "I must say, I'm happy you suggested we get together. I haven't heard very much from you since we started this little project which is not how I usually like to work with my consultants."

"Don't take it personally, Jon," Chris apologized. "I'm pretty independent by nature. You asked me to look after something, so I did. No sense bothering you every other day if I had nothing to deliver, right? Today, I have something for you."

He proceeded to recount, in fine detail, the events of the preceding week, from his witnessing Greg and Wayne's visit to pick up the wooden cases, to this morning's conversation where Wayne and Bryan had informed Greg of Bob's untimely passing.

After having spoken for an hour, during which time Jonathan had not uttered a sound, Chris concluded his report with a slight grin.

"That's what I've been up to, boss. How do you like my story?"

"It's definitely a good story, Chris," approved Jonathan, impressed by the progress his new recruit had made in just over a week. "Any suggestions as to where it goes from here?"

"I think that enough information has been accumulated to dump the whole thing on the police and have them handle it." Chris suggested. "They'll have names, dates, places, financial records, everything."

"Does that fit with our hero's regular pattern?" Jonathan queried with a smile. "Wouldn't he have some kind of internal drive to eliminate these assholes himself?"

"I've retired from my Vigilante days," Chris quietly replied. "I'm healed, remember? I'm willing to help my country, for a fee, but I've realized that I can't single-handedly wipe out crime. Bottom line, it's no longer my job, Jonathan."

Addley nodded thoughtfully, now convinced beyond a doubt that Chris was as sane as they came. His violent past had existed for reasons which Jonathan could understand but Chris had completed his therapy and was now at peace. Enough had paid for his pain according to his terms.

"You're absolutely right, Chris," Jonathan stated. "We definitely have enough for the cops to take over. When can you get the disks and tapes to me?"

"I'll get everything together tomorrow and we can meet somewhere on Saturday. I'll give you call."

"That will be fine," answered Jonathan, waving at the waiter for the check. "I just want to say that you've done some incredible work. I hope that you'll consider taking on some other contracts in the future. It would be a shame to let your talents go to waste."

"I'm too young to completely retire," replied a smiling Chris. "I don't plan to go for any full-time jobs, but you can consider me as a free-lance consultant."

* * * *

"You wanted to see me?" asked Matt from the door of Wayne's office.

"Yeah, I did," Wayne responded, looking up from the report he was reading. "Come on in, Matt. Would you close the door behind you?"

"Sure, boss," Matt replied, complying with his superior's request before having a seat. "What's up?"

Matt was generally a nervous individual who did not function well under too much pressure. Wayne was therefore certain that if Matt knew anything, he would crack in no time.

"We've had a few problems that I need to bring you up to speed with," announced Wayne, almost kindly.

"What kind of problems?" asked Matt.

His usual worried look appeared but he did not seem uneasy.

"Yesterday, we discovered that Bob was the one who had stolen those four keys of coke on Saturday," stated Wayne, eyeing Matt carefully.

"What? That's impossible, Wayne," exclaimed Matt. "Bob wasn't even in town on Saturday. He was gone ice fishing."

"So I've heard," replied Wayne. "Maybe he came back for something."

"No, Wayne," insisted Matt. "A few of the guys out back were up there with him. They were joking around and talking about their trip on Monday morning when we got in. I'm sure Bob was up there for the week-end."

"O.K. then. Maybe he grabbed the coke on Monday when you guys went over to Rick's place," Wayne suggested, still intently watching his subordinate.

"No way," Matt argued. "I was with him the whole time."

"Are you sure, Matt?" questioned Wayne. "This is very important."

"Wayne, I tell you there's no way that Bob could've found the coke and taken it without my knowing," Matt insisted, "Absolutely not."

"Then, is there any way that he might have taken it and that you *were* aware of it, Matt?" enquired Wayne, staring at the young man through narrow eyes.

"What?" shouted Matt, jumping from his seat, his expression a mixture of fear, disbelief and anger. "Bob had nothing to do with that coke disappearing and neither did I."

"Calm down, Matt, and sit down," commanded Wayne, knowing that the younger man spoke the truth. "I had to check. Relax. I believe you."

Matt returned to his chair, breathing heavily, clenching and unclenching his fists with rage and frustration.

"What did you do with Bob?" he asked sullenly, staring blankly at the floor.

"Listen," said Wayne with a tone of finality. "An important customer told us Bob sold him the coke. We went to talk to Bob about it and found a big pile of cash. Everything fit. We had to take care of Bob. End of story."

"You killed Bob," Matt slowly mumbled, in a daze. "But you killed him for nothing."

"Maybe we did, maybe we didn't," replied Wayne, not willing to admit his error. "Regardless, we have to move on. We can't change anything."

"Well, I think it's wrong," Matt announced with a sudden strength in his voice. "Don't you understand? You killed Bob for nothing."

"Let's just get one thing straight, you little bastard," Wayne hissed angrily. "We're all in this together. Do you understand? That means we stick together and, if we have to, we go down together. You think about that real carefully, mister, because if I start getting the impression that I can't trust you anymore, Bob is gonna be the least of your worries. Got it? Now, get the hell outta here. I've got things to do."

* * * *

"What can I get you, sir?" politely enquired the barman at the Sheraton Hotel.

"White rum and Coke, please," replied Chris.

"Here you go, sir."

"Thanks."

"Thank-you, sir."

Drink in hand, Chris rejoined Paul Anderson, President of Andernet Communications, to resume their conversation. Peterson had been right about this Chamber of Commerce cocktail. In just under an hour, Chris had established three contacts with whom his consulting services showed definite promise.

"As I was saying," resumed Anderson. "The direction our firm is heading in is definitely an area where your knowledge and expertise could come in handy..."

As Anderson spoke, Chris noticed Tony Bradley, his warehouse lessor, enter the reception hall at the far end. Suddenly oblivious of what Anderson was saying, Chris watched as Bradley greeted a few acquaintances. The latter apparently asked a question to which one of his buddies replied by pointing to the bar located behind Chris and Anderson. Bradley smiled, turned and headed directly towards them.

As if suddenly remembering something, Chris stared at his watch and exclaimed, "My God. Look at the time. Paul, you'll have to excuse me. I have an appointment downtown at 6:30. I have your card. I'll give you a call."

With that, he rushed off to a nearby exit, hoping that Bradley would not see him. He made it safely to door and quickly left the hotel, cursing himself for his renewed stupidity.

This game was nearly over. Now was not the time to make such careless mistakes.

* * * *

As Tony Bradley approached the bar, he caught a glimpse of Chris heading towards an exit.

"Hey, Mr. Johnson," he called out just as Chris was going through the doorway.

He hurried after Chris, but could not see him anywhere in the lobby beyond. He re-entered the hall and went to the bar to get himself a drink.

"Howya doin, Tony?" Wayne heartily enquired, sauntering up to join the warehouse owner.

He had witnessed Chris' sudden departure as well as Bradley's subsequent pursuit.

"I saw you running out there and thought you were leaving."

"Nah," Tony explained. "I was just trying to catch up with this guy I rented a warehouse to last week. Mr. Johnson. You know him?"

"Johnson? Johnson?" mused Wayne, deep in thought. "Don't believe I do. What's he look like?"

"Did you see the guy that walked out just before I did?" asked Tony.

"Blonde fellow?"

"Yeah, that's the guy," replied Tony. "That's Johnson. So, you know him?"

"Nope. Can't say that I do," answered Wayne, a slight smile on his lips. "He looks familiar though. What kind of business is he in?"

"Couldn't tell you," was Bradley's response. "All I know is that the guy rented one of my mini-warehouses to store some stuff and paid me ahead, three months, cash. My kinda guy."

"I guess," agreed Wayne with a knowing chuckle. "I just can't remember where I've seen him. Maybe I saw him roaming around your place."

"Could be," Tony answered. "He took the last warehouse in the building; the one that gives right by your yard."

"Yeah, that must be where I saw him," nodded Wayne. "Well, I'm gonna mingle. Catch you later, Tony."

* * * *

Chris settled back in the couch to watch Letterman with Sandy. Although the show was generally good every night, this evening's programme would be particularly appealing as the musical guest was Melissa Etheridge, of whom both Chris and Sandy were major fans.

As Letterman started his monologue, the phone rang.

"Who's calling at this time?" asked Sandy as Chris reached for the cordless on the couch beside him.

"Hello. Hello?"

The line went dead.

"Guess they didn't want to talk to me," shrugged Chris, tossing the phone back onto the couch.

"Unknown name, unknown number," stated Sandy, verifying the call display screen on the phone's base.

"Either a wrong number or one of your lovers," quipped Chris.

"Probably one of my lovers," agreed a smiling Sandy.

* * * *

Wayne cut the connection on his cellular phone and looked up at Bryan.

"Well, Mr. Johnson is home, so let's check out his warehouse."

They climbed out of Wayne's Jag and crossed the rear yard of Quality Imports towards the neighbouring warehouse building.

"How do you plan to get in there?" asked Bryan as they approached the door to Chris's warehouse.

"Our friend, Mr. Bradley, has an incredible love for money," Wayne smugly replied. "I rented the key to Barry's warehouse for the night for two hundred bucks. Another hundred bought me Bradley's promise to shut up."

He finished speaking as they reached the door and, after scanning the area to make sure they were alone, attempted to insert the key into the lock.

"Sonovabitch," he muttered under his breath.

"What's the matter?" asked Bryan.

"Either Bradley screwed me or that bastard Barry changed the fucking locks." Wayne hissed through clenched teeth.

He hurried over to the doors of the next two warehouses and verified the locks.

"The others are Weisers," he fumed as he returned. "This is a Medeco."

He peered at the key in his hand and added, "This key's a Weiser. Barry changed the locks."

"So, genius, now what?" taunted Bryan.

"We go get a ladder and break a fucking window on the second floor," Wayne shot back. "That's what, asshole."

Chapter 18 - Friday, January 31, 1997

It was 6:48 a.m. when Greg pulled into the parking lot of the Ste-Rose Diner. Getting up early was not one of his favourite sports, and doing so to have breakfast with Wayne and Bryan did little to render the activity more pleasurable. However, Wayne had sounded serious when he had called the previous night, or rather, very early that morning, and Greg had promised to meet them for breakfast at 6:30. At least, he had the satisfaction of arriving late.

After parking his car in the closest spot he could find, he hurried through the morning's bitter cold and entered the restaurant.

"Those bastards better be here," he muttered to himself, searching the dining hall for his two associates.

"Greg, back here," he heard, then saw, Wayne calling and waving from a booth in the rear corner.

He reached the table and was greeted with Wayne's "You're late," as he slid into the booth.

"I'm early enough," he grunted back, signalling a waitress by pointing to his coffee cup. "What's so goddamn urgent that it couldn't wait until a reasonable hour at the office?"

"We've got a problem," Bryan glumly announced.

"Yeah? Well, it seems every time we talk lately, we've got a problem," Greg whined. "What is it this time? Your friend Jimmy rip us off with the coke?"

"No," Bryan answered, realizing that they hadn't told Greg about that problem yet. "But that deal didn't completely pan out. Someone switched part of the shipment on us. Seven keys were powdered sugar when we delivered to Jimmy. He was not a happy man."

"Holy shit," whispered Greg, his grumpy disposition changing to one of fear. "You think it was Bob?"

"Actually, we're pretty sure that it wasn't Bob, or Matt," Wayne informed him, "In fact, we probably whacked Bob for nothing."

"Oh, great," Greg buried his face into his hands. "Then, what's going on? Who's doing this?"

"We think it's Chris Barry," Wayne hesitantly responded. "You were right, Greg," he added, not allowing his accountant friend the pleasure of saying 'I told you so.'.

"What led you geniuses to believe that Barry might not be trustworthy?" enquired Greg, his tone heavy with sarcasm.

"Yesterday, at the cocktail party, I saw our neighbour, Tony Bradley, running after Barry," answered Wayne, ignoring Greg's shot. "Only, Tony knew our friend by the name of Johnson. It seems that Mister Johnson rented one of Tony's mini-warehouses to store a bunch of stuff. Now, it turns out that the warehouse in question, which happens to overlook the back of our building, is empty. Anyways, now it is. Until last night, this was stored in there, right by the window that gives on our yard."

He placed a video cam on the table before him.

"The bastard's been filming us?" whispered Greg incredulously.

"It would seem so," Wayne nodded. "When we got into his warehouse last night, the camera was running. The only thing is, there was no tape in it. It's probably got some kinda transmitter set in it or something."

"Jesus Christ," Greg swore, visibly shaken. "Do you think he knows we're onto him?"

Wayne was unable to hold off a grin. "Well, if he was filming last night, he'll know as soon as he looks at the tape. The sonovabitch changed the locks on the doors so we couldn't get in with the keys I got from Tony. We get a ladder and Bryan climbs up to the window on the second floor. He trying to see something inside and has got his face pressed up against the glass. He notices a small red light glowing right inside and suddenly realizes that he's got a camera lens about six inches from his mug. He nearly fell off the ladder. I never thought somebody Bryan's size could move that quick."

"Yeah, yeah, real funny, asshole," muttered Bryan. "Next time you go up and we'll see how you do."

Turning his attention to Greg, he continued. "We think that Barry might have bugged our offices and phones. That would explain how he knew about the dope, the deliveries, so on and so forth; which means, we don't talk at the office anymore until we fix this guy."

"And how do we plan to go about that?" Greg asked, once again wishing he had never gotten into this business.

"Presuming that he hasn't seen last night's tape yet, he'll be in the office this morning," Wayne hopefully replied. "If that's the case, we'll invite him to lunch and stash him somewhere until we figure out what to do."

"But what if he has seen the tape?" Greg insisted. "What then?"

"Then we'll go over to his place and have a chat with him there," Wayne quietly stated. "Either way, this piece of shit is not going to fuck us up. We've come too far to have some righteous ex-executive take us down."

"What if he's not in this alone?" an ever-worrisome Greg pushed on. "What if he's a cop or something?"

"Oh, Jesus-Christ, Greg," Wayne retorted in frustration. "The guy's a well-known Montreal businessman whose been building his career for years. He's had his picture in the papers dozens of times in the last five years. All of that was just a set-up for some cop? Come on, get real."

"I guess you're right," Greg uneasily admitted. "It's just that things have been pretty screwy over the last three weeks and I'm getting really nervous."

"Relax, Greg. Take it easy," soothed Wayne. "We've identified the problem. Now we'll fix it and everything will go back to normal. Don't worry so much."

* * * *

"Good morning, gorgeous," Sandy greeted her husband as she joined him in the kitchen. "You're up bright and early."

"Yep. Got things to do, people to see," Chris replied, leaning back to kiss her. "Going to visit a friend of Jonathan's this morning. Apparently, the guy's got a fancy set-up to edit and copy videotapes. I can probably get what's important on one cassette."

"Are you getting everything to Jonathan today?" asked Sandy, anxious for her husband's spy adventure to end.

"Nah. More likely tomorrow," answered Chris. "I want to review the whole thing one last time before I deliver. I want to make sure my face or name don't appear anywhere in any incriminating fashion. What are you up to today?"

"Cathy's picking me up and we're heading downtown for lunch and a little bit of shopping. You need anything?"

"Nothing comes to mind," Chris responded with a smirk. "Anyways, you should start going easy on the spending. Don't forget that I'm no longer permanently employed."

"I promise to buy only what's on sale." laughed Sandy.

* * * *

"The bastard's not coming in," Wayne announced to Greg and Bryan.

They were standing in an open area of the shipping department, relatively comfortable that they were safe from bugs.

"Maybe he's just late," suggested Greg hopefully.

"No such luck," Wayne sneered. "I spoke to Peterson. Barry called him earlier to say that he had some personal business to attend to. Maybe he'll come in this afternoon but he said not to expect him."

"So, now what?" asked a nervous Greg, sweat starting to trickle down his back.

"So now, Bryan and I will pay Mister Barry a visit," Wayne replied. "I told Peterson that we would be visiting customers all day. Greg, you stay here. If anything strange happens or if Barry shows up, call us."

"I don't like this," muttered Greg, wringing his hands. "It's all gonna blow up in our faces."

"Not if we move fast," Wayne insisted impatiently. "Just stay calm and keep your eyes open. We'll fix this. Let's go, Bryan."

* * * *

A few years earlier, Sandy had taken up oil painting as a pastime. Since, her easels remained installed in permanence in one corner of the sunroom, with never less than two canvasses in the making. It was a hobby which she truly enjoyed and she often picked up brush and palette as soon as five or more minutes of free time became available.

Cathy was to pick her up around 10 o'clock and it was only 9:45. With fifteen minutes ahead of her, she headed for the sunroom to pursue her latest masterpiece. No sooner had she entered the room than the doorbell rang.

"Cathy's early," she said aloud as she returned to the front of the house to greet her friend.

She opened the door and was startled to find herself faced by two gentlemen, both who looked vaguely familiar.

"Yes, can I help you?" she asked, trying to remember where she had seen these men before.

"Is Mister Barry home?" queried Bryan, pleasantly enough.

"No," replied Sandy, suddenly wary of the two individuals standing before her. "Unfortunately he's not. If you want to leave your names, I'll be sure to let him know you dropped by."

"Where is he?" demanded Wayne, not as pleasantly as his counterpart.

"He's not here," retorted Sandy, raising her tone. "Now, if you gentlemen will excuse me, I'm busy," she added as she started to close the door.

With a swift gesture, Wayne straight-armed the door, slamming it open and causing Sandy to jump back in astonishment.

"Not so fast, lady," he snarled, moving inside, followed by Bryan. "We ain't done talking yet."

"I don't know who the hell you think you are," screamed Sandy, regaining her composure. "But you better get the hell out of here."

"Shut up, bitch," growled Wayne as Bryan closed the front door behind them. "Now, where the fuck is Barry."

"I don't know," Sandy coldly responded, hiding her fear. "He must be at work."

"No," replied Bryan in his annoyingly pleasant voice. "If he was there, we wouldn't have had to come over here and bother you sweetheart, now, would we?"

"W-well, then I can't help you," stammered Sandy, suddenly recognizing her visitors. "If he's not at work, then I don't know where he is."

"O.K." sneered Wayne. "Then, here's what we're gonna do. Let's the three of us go for a ride. Later, if you remember where Chris is, you can let us know. Get your coat Mrs. Barry. It's cold out there."

* * * *

"McCall, Homicide," Dave answered the phone.

"Hi, hon," said Cathy, his wife. "Sorry to bother you."

"No problem. What's up?"

"Well, I'm parked outside at Sandy's and Chris' place," Cathy replied with concern. "Sandy and I were supposed to go shopping together but nobody's home."

140

"You sure it was today?" asked Dave.

"Of course I'm sure," answered Cathy. "I spoke to Sandy yesterday afternoon. I tried her cellular but it's not on. Do you have Chris' number with you? I'd call him to make sure everything's all right."

"Yeah, hang on a second," her husband replied, digging into his briefcase. "Here we go. You can reach him at 668-1245 at work. I'll give you his cell phone too; 352-3310. If anything's wrong, let me know."

"I will," Cathy promised. "Thanks. Love you, and be careful. Bye."

* * * *

Chris was quite impressed with the video equipment made available by Sonny, Jonathan's acquaintance. In just over two hours, he had managed to edit a week's worth of videotapes onto one cassette, thanks to Sonny's miniature audio-visual recording studio.

He was rapid-viewing the final cassette, that from the previous night, when his cell phone rang.

"Hello," he replied, his eyes glued to the images moving at high speed on the monitor before him.

"Hi, Chris," he heard Cathy McCall's voice on the line. "How are you?"

"Fine, Cathy, fine. Yourself?"

"Doing O.K., thanks. Chris, do you know where your lovely wife is?"

"I thought you two were going to spend Dave's and my hard earned money?" Chris jokingly replied. "Why? Where are you?"

"In your driveway," Cathy answered. "Sandy doesn't seem to be home."

"That's strange," Chris responded, puzzled. "I know she didn't forget that you were going out together because she talked about it this morning. Maybe she just went out to run a quick errand."

"Probably," agreed Cathy. "I'll wait a bit. If you hear from her, you can reach me in my car."

"O.K.," Chris replied, a little concerned. "Let me know if she doesn't show up."

"I will. Don't worry. Bye."

Chris flipped the phone shut and laid it down on the counter beside him, looking away from the video monitor for a second or two. As he returned his attention to the screen, he had the impression of having caught a glimpse of a face just before the image disappeared, to be replaced by the hissing snow of an unrecorded tape.

He pressed the rewind button and, sure enough, the face appeared again, but only for a fraction of a second at such a high speed. Curious and anxious, he hit the play button on the control panel before him and the tape began playing normally. He could see the deserted back lot of Quality Imports and not much else.

But wait. He detected a slight movement in the darkness at the bottom of the screen. He re-winded again and resumed his viewing at normal speed. He could vaguely make out two men walking in the dark towards Quality Imports, apparently coming from Bradley's warehouse. As they moved into the light of the Quality building, Chris easily recognized Wayne and Bryan.

As he watched, he saw Wayne enter the building's shipping area and return with a ladder which he handed down to Bryan. The latter hurried back towards Bradley's building, followed by Wayne and soon, both men were out of the camera's scope.

Several seconds later, a few dull, metallic clanking sounds were heard, followed by the sudden close-up appearance of Bryan's pudgy face, inches from the camera lens. No more than another half-minute went by before the sound of breaking glass could be heard, after which, the image completely disappeared.

They had discovered him, or at least his camera. But how? Probably thanks to Tony Bradley, although Chris didn't really hold the warehouse owner responsible. It was his own stupidity that had led to his being found out.

Anyways, it didn't really matter. He'd get everything together and make his delivery to Jonathan today. If required, he and Sandy would spend the weekend safely out of town.

Sandy? Where was she? It was not like her to be late for an appointment. She had too much respect for people.

His stomach tightened as he grabbed for his phone and speed-dialled their home number. No answer. He tried her cell phone but got the network's message centre indicating that the user was currently not available.

Was it possible that they had gotten hold of Sandy? He'd never forgive himself if something happened to her, especially if it was a result of his own carelessness.

He decided to call Cathy back, hoping that Sandy had since arrived. As he flipped open his phone, it rang, startling him.

"Hello?" he answered.

"Hi, Chris," Sandy's voice sounded strained.

"Hi! Where are you? What's the matter?" he asked, both relieved and concerned.

"She's with some friends, Mr. Johnson," Wayne's familiar voice chided, making Chris feel nauseous.

"You're making a serious mistake, Wayne," Chris responded, his voice deadly quiet.

"No. You made a serious mistake, Barry," Wayne shouted into the phone. "We weren't looking for any trouble. This is your fault. You fuck with us, you pay."

"Listen to me very carefully, Wayne," Chris continued softly. "Take very good care of my wife. It will make your death much less painful."

"Chris, Chris, Chris," taunted Wayne in a soothing tone. "You're really not in any position to make threats right now. Don't worry about your dear little wife. She's just collateral. Nothing'll happen to her as long as you're a good boy. Now, I just wanted to let you know that she was with us. I'll call you back later. In the meantime, be a smart boy. O.K.?"

With that, the line went dead.

Chris stared at the phone in his hand, breathing deeply to ease the churning he felt inside. After several moments, having somewhat regained his composure, he punched in Cathy's number and waited impatiently for her to pick up.

"Yeah, Cathy? Chris. Listen, Sandy just gave me a call. She wasn't feeling well and decided to go to the clinic. No, nothing serious. Don't worry. Yeah, I'll have her call you. Sorry you drove out for nothing. No, I don't think we can make it this weekend. I'm gonna be really busy. Listen, I have to go. I'll ask Sandy to call you later, O.K.? Once again, sorry. Bye."

* * * *

At 5:26, Dave McCall pulled into the driveway of his Dorval home, trying to remember the last time he had left work at a reasonable hour. Smiling,

144

he climbed out of the car and headed into the house, looking forward to a complete weekend off with Cathy.

"Hi, hon," he called from the foyer as he peeled off the apparel necessary for Montreal winters.

"Hey there," exclaimed Cathy, coming down the stairs. "This is a pleasant surprise."

"Yup," replied Dave. "And if all goes well, nobody's gonna kill anybody over the weekend and you'll have to endure me for the next two days."

"I think I can manage that," she murmured, placing her arms around his neck and kissing him.

"So, did you and Sandy have a good time?" asked Dave as they moved into the kitchen.

"Actually, we didn't go. Sandy wasn't feeling well and was gone to the clinic when I got there. Chris got back to me to let me know after I called him."

"Anything serious?" enquired Dave, concerned.

"I guess not," Cathy shrugged. "At least Chris didn't think so. He said that Sandy would call me back but I haven't heard from her. I'll give her a shout tomorrow."

"If they're up to it, maybe we can get together."

"Well, I suggested that to Chris but he said he'd be really busy this weekend," Cathy replied. She hesitated a little, then added, "Chris sounded strange when I spoke to him, Dave. He seemed distant and anxious to get off the phone. I had the impression something was wrong."

"You just worry too much, Mother," Dave kidded. "He was probably just worried about Sandy."

"I guess," Cathy doubtfully replied. "I just had a feeling that there was a problem."

"We'll talk to them tomorrow and you'll see, everything will be all right. Now, let's get something to eat. I'm starving."

* * * *

He pulled on some black jeans and a sweat-shirt, also black, found his running shoes and put them on. He moved downstairs to the hall closet where he pulled out his black leather jacket. Black leather gloves and a baseball cap completed his outfit.

He headed into the dining room where the apparatus required for the evening lay on the table. As he reviewed the items one last time, he wondered if his true intention had ever been to retire from his violent activities. If so, why had he kept all this equipment? Souvenirs?

He completed his inventory check and was comfortable that he had everything he might need. The two handguns went on his person, the .357 Magnum in the holster strapped under his right arm, the other, a tiny .22, into a small discreet pocket within his jacket. The switchblade went into a zippered pocket on the left leg of his jeans. The rest; tape, rope, wire snips, and a few lock picking devices, went into a small gym bag.

He knew that he wouldn't have to worry about an alarm system. He had checked that afternoon and the home he was planning to visit was linked with Pro-Tek Systems. A little computer hacking had ensured that the system would be properly dysfunctional.

He headed towards the garage, pausing only to pick up the new baseball bat he had purchased that afternoon, cash.

He started up the Pathfinder and rolled down the driveway, heading for his destination. As he reached the street, the phone rang on the seat beside him.

"Hello?"

"Chris," greeted Jonathan's voice. "I hadn't heard from you today so I was wondering what was going on? Are we still on for tomorrow?"

"No," was Chris's blunt reply.

"No? What do you mean, no? What's the matter, Chris?"

"This thing has become personal, Jonathan."

"Personal?" exclaimed Jonathan, angry and bewildered. "Chris, what the hell is going on? Have you lost it? I thought the 'Vigilante' had retired?"

"They found me out and took Sandy, Jonathan," Chris stonily replied. "It's become personal."

"Ah Jesus," Jonathan muttered in disgust. "I'm sorry, Chris. When did this happen?"

"This morning around ten. They called me and told me to lay off. They're supposed to call me back but I don't know when."

"Why didn't you call me, Chris?" Jonathan reproached. "I can help. You know that. I've got a whole team if we need it."

"This is personal and I intend to make these bastards pay, Jonathan," Chris coldly stated. "You've got to understand that."

"I understand, and believe me, they'll pay. I'm not suggesting that you let us take over, Chris. I'm telling you, let us help. Let *me* help."

Chris was silent for a moment before responding. "I'll think about it. Right now, I've got an errand to run. I'll give you a call when I get back."

"Are you sure, Chris? Don't bullshit me."

"I'll call you, Jonathan," Chris promised. "Some time tonight. Maybe late but I'll call."

"All right, Chris," Jonathan sighed. "Be careful."

"I will. Thanks, Jon."

* * * *

Matt poured himself another healthy dose of vodka, splashing some on the counter in the process, but not caring. What was this? Drink number five, number six? It didn't matter. What mattered was the numbness. At least the nausea was gone and the buzz felt good. But he still wished he had never gotten into this.

Sure, at first, and for a while, it was a blast. He was important, he had money, his friends admired him and he was respected at the clubs and restaurants he frequented; life in the fast lane, Mister Big Shot. That was all fine and nice until they shot George. And everything had turned to shit since. Now it was kidnapping on top of the drugs and murders. And Wayne, the genius, had no idea who Chris Barry even was or what he knew. The guy might be a goddamn cop. And to top it all, they were now holding Barry's wife at his, Matt's, cottage in St-Sauveur.

Feeling another bout of nausea coming on, Matt went for the vodka again, not bothering with a glass this time. The burn felt good and his stomach settled once more.

As he put the bottle back down, the phone rang, startling him. He hoped, prayed, that it wouldn't be Wayne. At least, with half a bottle of vodka and a few snorts of coke in him, he'd have a good excuse not to go if they asked him to head to the cottage that night.

"Yeah?" he mumbled into the phone, the drugs and alcohol really starting to take their toll.

"Hello, Mister Shaffer, please," asked the voice on the phone.

"Listen, bud," slurred Matt. "This is the third time I tell you. There's no fucking Mr. Shaffer here. Understand?"

"I'm sorry to have bothered you, sir," the voice apologized. "I promise I won't call again."

* * * *

Outside Matt's house, Chris flipped his phone shut and pulled the wire snips from his gym bag.

"Just wanna make sure that you won't call anybody either, you little piece of shit," he breathed as he severed the home's phone line.

He crept along the shovelled patio and up the steps leading to the elevated terrace from where he had a view of the kitchen inside. As he watched, he saw Matt sitting at the dining room table beyond, apparently preparing a line of coke.

"I better get in there soon," he muttered as he crawled back down the steps. "Bastard's gonna kill himself without any help."

He headed for a pair of french doors located at patio level and peered inside at what seemed to be a game room of sorts; pool table, bar, big screen T.V. A quick examination of the lock confirmed that this would be his point of entry. As long as Matt remained in the upper section of the split-level house, he wouldn't hear a thing.

He got to work on the lock and, within ten seconds, felt the bolt slide back. Pushing the door in no more than half an inch, he reached into the gym bag, pulled out an aerosol can of lubricant and quickly sprayed the hinge areas of the door. He'd been careless enough in recent days; no more.

Moving soundlessly into the dark room, he headed toward a dimly lit corridor atop a short flight of stairs. Upon reaching the top step, he looked down the hall to his left, towards the kitchen and dining room. He could see Matt, back to him, still sitting at the table, still playing with his little pile of white powder.

He crept slowly, silently, one step at a time, praying for the floorboards to remain quiet under the thick carpet as he approached his unsuspecting prey. He reached Matt just as the latter bent forward for a snort. As the young man regained his original position, he felt something cold and hard press into the back of his neck.

"Do not make any sudden moves, Matt," Chris ordered in a gentle voice. "If you do, I will blow your throat out. Nod slightly if you understand."

The nod was barely perceptible.

"Good. Now, I want you to bring your arms down along the sides of the back of your chair. Slowly, that's good. You and I are going to get along great, Matt; real rapport."

He proceeded to heavily tape Matt's wrists to the top of the chair's rear legs.

"Now, your feet, Matt. Great. I don't even have to tell you what to do. You're a natural. There you go. All taped up."

He walked into the kitchen and closed the vertical blinds.

"Wouldn't want the neighbours peeking in on us," said Chris, winking at Matt as he pulled out a chair and sat down. "Now, let's you and I have a little chat, O.K.?"

Matt nodded, his eyes uncertain.

"I guess you know who I am, Matt? You've seen me around the warehouse, haven't you?"

Matt nodded again.

"You can answer me, Matt," encouraged Chris, lightly patting the young man's cheek. "You can talk. I want you to talk, O.K.?"

"Y-yes sir," Matt mumbled.

"Good, Matt. Good. And you can call me Chris. None of this sir bullshit; I don't function well under formality. Now, what should we talk about? Do you have any ideas?"

"N-no, Chris."

"No? Well, here's something we can talk about. Why don't you tell me where you cocksuckers are holding my wife. Let's start with that, Matt."

"I-I don't know where she is. They didn't tell me. They just said that I should stay home and wait til they called."

"Wrong answer, Matt," Chris barked, his tone much colder. "Try again."

"I swear, Chris," Matt insisted, suddenly feeling strangely sober. "Wayne called me and told me that they had grabbed your wife and that he'd call me later. That's all I know."

Chris leaned across the table, his face inches from his prisoner's. "Are you sure you don't know anything else, Matt?"

"I swear, man. If I did, I'd tell you."

"Let me think about that, Matt," Chris mused as he picked up his roll of filament tape, cutting off a six inch strip.

"W-what are you doing?"

"I need a bit of peace and quiet while I think," Chris explained as he applied the tape firmly to Matt's mouth.

He paced around the room for a moment before turning back towards the young man.

"Maybe you're telling me the truth, Matt. But, maybe you're not. You see, I have a hard time believing little, motherfucker, drug pushing, murderer, pricks like you. So I have to be convinced that you're not lying to me."

He turned and moved into the kitchen where he began opening drawers from which he selected several cooking utensils. Matt watched, his terror mounting, as Chris turned on the two front burners of the gas range and proceeded to place the variety of knives, forks, spatulas and other cooking tools in the flames.

"This," said Chris approvingly, holding up a potato masher before placing it on the burner, "Can be a lot of fun. You've got some nice stuff here, Matt. Nothing like heat resistant handles on cooking utensils. I hate burning myself. Don't you?"

He examined his lay-out on the stove and, satisfied, returned to his chair facing Matt.

"We'll let those heat up for a few minutes, get them nice and hot. In the meantime, you might want to think real hard about where my wife is."

* * * *

As Chris approached his home, he noticed a dark Acura Vigor parked in the driveway, close to the house and facing the street. He slowed and watched, waiting for the signal. Two quick flashes of the headlights, followed by a pause; then three longer flashes. As he pulled into the driveway, he activated the automated garage door and signalled the driver of the Acura to back into the three car garage. He followed, pulling in between the Acura and his Lexus.

"Greetings," said Jonathan as he got out of his car. "How are you holding up?"

"O.K. so far," Chris sombrely replied. "I'll be a lot better when Sandy's back and I've taken care of these bastards."

"Don't worry, Chris," Jonathan responded in a determined tone. "That'll be **real** soon. Have they contacted you again?"

"Nope. Not yet. And that's got me worried."

"Don't be," reassured Jonathan. "They're still trying to figure out their next step which I'm sure is not real clear in their minds right now."

"Well, let's get going," replied Chris. "Because I'm pretty clear what my next steps are gonna be."

They moved into the house from the garage, pursuing their conversation as they went along.

"So, how did your errand go?" Jonathan asked, not knowing exactly where Chris had been but certain that it was linked to the whole affair.

"Exactly as planned," responded Chris with fire in his eyes. "Now I know where they're holding her and I have a pretty good idea who's there."

"Who'd you visit?" enquired Jonathan.

"Matt, one of their gofers," answered Chris, "The one who was still alive."

"Was?" Jonathan raised an eyebrow. "Nobody saw you?"

"No. Being careless is what got Sandy involved in this thing. I'm not careless anymore."

"Good," said Jonathan. "What's next on your agenda?"

"Greg Pierce, the accountant," Chris replied. "I'm gonna visit him to make sure we have his complete journal. Then I'll make sure that he doesn't interfere with the rest of our week-end plans."

"When are you going to see him?"

"Early in the morning," answered Chris. "After that, you and I head up to Matt's chalet in St-Sauveur."

"Who's going to be there?"

"As far as Matt could tell me, Wayne and Bryan are up there," replied Chris. "They've also asked their friend, Diamond Jimmy, for some help. They should have four members of the Aces of Death guarding the place. Matt was supposed to drive up there in the morning but, unfortunately, he's not gonna be able to make it."

"So we'll have to move quickly," stated Jonathan. "Before they find out what happened to Matt. Are you sure that Matt told you the truth about where they're holding Sandy?"

"Yeah," Chris nodded. "I convinced him that if he didn't play straight with me, I'd hurt him really bad. He even gave me the blueprints of his St-Sauveur place. I'm sure that he told me the truth."

He stood up and stretched as he looked at the clock on the wall. "It's quarter to one. I'm going to catch a couple of hours of sleep. Make yourself at home and holler if you need anything. The guest room is the first door to the right upstairs when you want to get some sleep."

"I'm fine for now," Jonathan replied. "I treated myself to a little nap while I was waiting for your call. I'd like to see the information you collected, if you don't mind, and I might have a few calls make."

"Second door to the right upstairs is my study," offered Chris. "There's a phone, PC, fax and anything else you might need. You'll find two boxes on the table in the corner. Everything's in there, including seven kilos of cocaine. Enjoy yourself. I'll see you in a couple of hours."

Chapter 19 - Saturday, February 1, 1997

Greg turned over in his sleep, trying to escape the annoying sound, but it persisted. He awoke to realize that the phone was ringing. As he sat up in his bed, he squinted at his watch and swore.

"Hello," he growled into the phone.

"Greg, where the fuck is Matt?" shouted an angry Wayne on the other end of the line.

"Jesus, Wayne, how am I supposed to know?" retorted Greg. "It's not even goddamn five o'clock. I was sleeping."

"Yeah, well, get up," ordered Wayne. "I told that little bastard to stay home until I called him. Now there's no answer. I want you to get over to his place and make sure everything's O.K. I don't trust that little scumbag. I think he's really starting to lose it and I don't want him running to the cops. Call me back once you know what's going on."

With that, the phone went dead in Greg's hand.

"Goddamn Jesus fucking Christ," Greg shrieked as he climbed out of bed and started getting dressed to go to Matt's place. "This is gonna have to end soon."

* * * *

Chris approached Greg's residence which was located just a few blocks from Matt's, where he'd been the night before. As he turned onto the accountant's street, he spotted the latter's Buick Roadmaster pull out of the driveway and speed away. He accelerated a little and proceeded to tail the large car. It quickly became obvious that Greg was on his way to Matt's, where they arrived within a matter of minutes, Greg parking in the driveway while Chris stopped half a dozen houses away to watch.

Greg climbed out of the car and hurried to the front door of the attractive home, clearly unaware that he had been followed. He rang then pulled a key from his coat pocket, unlocked the front door and went inside, closing the door behind him. Less than a minute later, the door was thrown open and Greg rushed out, barely managing to make it down the five steps leading to the driveway before falling to his knees and vomiting what was left of his prior evening's dinner.

He remained on his knees for a few seconds, breathing heavily, before standing up again, unsteadily. With an air of panic, he glanced wildly about, trying to determine if anyone had seen him. Barring an unoccupied Pathfinder parked further down the street, the area was deserted.

He stumbled hurriedly back up the steps to close the door, not bothering to lock it, and rushed back to his car. He backed out of the driveway and headed back for home as quickly as he could without squealing the tires. In his frenzied state, he did not notice the Pathfinder leave the curb to follow him.

* * * *

The small conference room at the RCMP Quebec Division office in downtown Montreal slowly and quietly began to fill at 5:25 a.m. Ten people had been summoned and there was no doubt that all would show up.

There was little conversation as they arrived. Most were not scheduled to work that day and those who were, were only slated to start somewhat later. The eve being Friday, some had barely had time to fall asleep when the call had come.

Although the meeting had been called for 5:30, three of the participants had still not arrived at 5:35. At 5:37, one rushed in, looking like he had not even had the chance to get to bed from the night before. They had stressful jobs and liked to unwind on their nights off. Another arrived a moment later, the dishevelled hair indicating that some slumber had been attained, but the dark glasses highlighting that the previous evening had been demanding.

As was always the case when such a meeting was called, the last arrival was Nick Sharp, Director of the Quebec Division, RCMP, and caller of the meeting. Such tardiness was not of his usual nature and only occurred at these special meetings. He recognized that in such circumstances, these people were doing more, much more than they had signed up for when joining the force. They were the best he had and all dropped their personal schedules and lives without a word whenever required. He therefore always made sure that everyone was present before joining them at these meetings, allowing them the impression that none were late.

At 5:39, he entered the small conference room, greeting the ten seated around the cigarette scarred table as he closed the door.

"Good morning, ladies and gentlemen. I thank you all for being here on such short notice."

157

An array of nods, mumbles and grunts were offered in response.

"Good," Nick continued with a smile. "I can see that everyone's fully rested and raring to go."

This time, a medley of grunts, chuckles and mutterings emanated from around the table.

"Alright. Let's get rolling. A friend has supplied me with some very interesting information," Nick informed them, using the opening line he always used at such meetings. "In summary, we're dealing with some people who've been importing smack and coke from Thailand and Columbia using an honest import company as their means and cover. The Aces of Death have become their main client in recent weeks so we'll finally have a chance to get a crack at those bastards."

Murmurs of approval were pronounced from the rapidly wakening group.

"As in the past, we've been lucky enough to have a shit-load of data dumped onto us," Nick went on, "Without having to spend months following, investigating and tracking down a bunch of low-lives. So now, we have to shake our asses and put together some solid case files and investigation reports real quick. I trust that none of you had any major plans for the week-end?"

A combination of shrugs, moans and blasphemies came as response to the rhetorical question.

"No wonder I like working with you guys so much," Nick exclaimed. "As usual, the information that's been supplied is in its raw form. Some of it will have to be modified a little to make it stick. This story has to stand up when we're done with it if we want to cover for my friend out there. I've already got some points that we'll need to fine tune and he'll be getting back to me with some last minute details over the next day or two; Andy, John, Sue, Lisa and Gary, everything's in those two boxes."

He paused to light a cigarette before continuing.

"There's a dozen pages of notes in the top box that map out quite nicely how this whole thing might have taken place. Base yourself on that. If you have any questions, let me know. Now, go and write me an incredible story. Arty and the rest of you, stick around. We've got some visits to coordinate."

* * * *

Greg sat in his study, working feverishly on his journal. He'd had enough with the whole thing and had made a decision. Everything was falling apart and, in addition to possibly getting busted soon, his dying had now become a real possibility.

As soon as he completed this final entry he would take his precious journal, go hide somewhere and contact the cops. Once they promised immunity, he'd deliver, testify and disappear. He could definitely afford it financially and, since his wife had left him, he had no ties to hold him back.

He completed his entry and proceeded to save his document. Following the usual crunching of the hard drive, he was surprised to see the screen suddenly go completely black for a couple of seconds before turning bright red.

"What the fuck?" he muttered under his breath, dumbfounded.

He hoped that nothing was wrong with his computer. He hadn't backed up his data in quite a while and now was not the time for his journal to become inaccessible. He tried hitting a few keys but generated no reaction from the machine. As he was about to attempt to reboot the system, bold black letters began to appear on the red screen.

IT'S OVER GREG. YOU AND YOUR FRIENDS HAVE GONE TOO FAR. DON'T THINK YOU CAN DO ANYTHING WITH YOUR JOURNAL. IT'S GONE. NOW, YOU MUST DIE. YOU SAW WHAT HAPPENED TO MATT. THAT WAS NOTHING. HE WAS JUST A JUNIOR IN YOUR OPERATION. NOT YOU. YOU'RE ONE OF THE BIG BOYS. THAT MEANS YOU REALLY GET TO SUFFER AS YOU GO. IN A VERY SHORT WHILE, YOU WILL WISH THAT YOU HAD BEEN ARRESTED AND THROWN INTO PRISON FOR LIFE. GETTING SODOMIZED EVERY NIGHT BY A DIFFERENT SLIME BAG WOULD BE PARADISE COMPARED TO THE TORTURE I WILL MAKE YOU ENDURE. I WILL TEND TO YOU SOON (SOONER THAN YOU THINK).

As each word appeared, painfully slowly, letter by letter, Greg read the message with growing terror. Although he had emptied his stomach in Matt's front yard, he found himself retching uncontrollably. Sweat poured out of every pore of his body and within a matter of moments, his clothes were soaked through. Glancing down for an instant, he had the faint realization that he had urinated in his pants.

The message finally finished printing itself on the screen, glaringly taunting the accountant. Greg stared back, in a daze.

After a minute or two, he reached down to the lower drawer of his desk, pulling it open in a slow, mechanical fashion. He absently pulled out the .

38 Special which Wayne had given him two years earlier, stuck the barrel into his mouth and pulled the trigger.

* * * *

After making sure that he had in fact copied the final version of Greg's journal, Chris snapped his notepad closed and slipped it back into his duffel bag.

Quietly, he climbed the stairs leading from the basement of Greg's home to the first floor. As far as he could determine from Greg's steps earlier, the study would be at the back of the house, off to the left. He headed in that direction, gun in hand, alert for any possible danger, although he didn't expect any. He had heard the shot a moment earlier.

Before actually reaching the room, he could see through the open door that Greg would present no immediate or eventual threat to himself or anyone else. The man had, wisely, literally blown his brains out.

Chris leaned over the dead accountant's body and rebooted the PC. Only a few seconds were required to confirm that he had in fact erased the journal from the hard drive.

"Bye, Greg," he said softly as he headed for the basement door by which he had entered. As he descended the stairs, he could hear the phone begin to ring upstairs.

* * * *

"Jesus Christ! Stupid motherfuckers," Wayne screamed hysterically, throwing the cordless phone across the room. "Where the fuck are those assholes?"

"Calm down, Wayne, Jesus," snapped Bryan, his tone exasperated. "Maybe they went to get something to eat. What the fuck is your problem?"

"I told that idiot, Matt, that I would call," Wayne hissed impatiently. "And I asked that other goddamn moron to call me once he had checked in on Matt. That ain't that complicated, Bryan. Why didn't they call? Something's wrong. I know it."

"I'll go check," Bryan decided, lifting his bulky form from the couch. "I'm getting tired of sitting around here anyways, seeing as you don't want me to party with our little friend upstairs."

"We don't touch her until we've figured out exactly what to do. Understand?" commanded Wayne. "Once we get our hands on Barry, you can do whatever you want with her. Not before."

"Yeah, yeah. I know," Bryan rolled his eyes, having heard the speech several times already. "The more I wait, the sweeter she'll be. Anyways, I'm gonna go see what's up with Greg and Matt. And don't worry. *I'll* call."

* * * *

Andy Kovac had never dreamed that working as a clerk for a customs broker would prove to be such a lucrative position. And to think, four years earlier, he had come so close to quitting this dead-end job.

That had been right before Wayne had showed up and offered to pay a handsome salary for very little work. Just a little merchandise coordination at the warehouse until the proper customs inspectors came along. That was it.

And the nice thing was, his wife didn't even know about it. That meant that he got to spend all the extra cash on his greatest passion; sex with the hottest call girls in town; sometimes a nooner, other times, the always reliable 'night out with the boys'.

Last night had been particularly interesting, he thought as he stepped into the shower. With his wife gone to Vancouver to visit her sister, he had been able to hire not one or two, but three lovely and very nasty ladies to cater to his needs, right in the comfort of his own home. It had been expensive but, God, it had been worth it. He was surprised that he could even stand up this morning.

As he continued to think of the previous evening and the three women still sleeping in his bed, he found himself getting excited again. He looked down at his now semi-aroused penis and smiled.

"I'm so proud of you," he chuckled, now convinced that he'd be in shape for another round of fun and games.

As if in response to his desires, he heard someone come into the bathroom.

"I don't know who you are," he called out over the shower curtain. "But I've got one stiff cock here that needs some attention."

The shower curtain was pushed aside and he found himself staring at a very large gun, held by a very large man. Two uniformed officers stood in the background.

"Don't look that stiff to me, Andy," said Arty Hubbard of the RCMP. "Anyways, you're not really my type. I prefer long legs and breasts. Get your clothes on, Andy. We're going downtown. You're under arrest for conspiring to import illegal narcotics into the country. You have the right to retain and instruct counsel..."

* * * *

Richie 'Butch' Boulanger was only nineteen but he had already killed several times, even before the Aces of Death had asked him to do so to prove he was worthy of being a member. And he had proved it beyond the shadow of a doubt.

It was not simply that taking a life did not bother him. He actually enjoyed doing it. 'The ultimate power trip', he had bragged to others. Some of his associates thought that he was just a little too crazy. However, all treated him with respect and few dared to confront him when disagreements arose. It was thanks to Richie's fearless qualities that Diamond Jimmy had selected him as one of the four guards to help out Wayne and Bryan.

* * * *

Jimmy had not been happy when Wayne had called but the quality of the dope these idiots were supplying him with warranted a little patience towards their inexperience in the field of illegal narcotics. He just hoped that they would improve with time.

Actually, what Jimmy was really banking on was that Wayne et al. stay in business just long enough for the Aces of Death to develop the direct contacts with the suppliers in Asia and Columbia. After that, Wayne and his little friends would become expendable. After that, they would become useless.

* * * *

Richie had been assigned to guard the sector to the east of Matt's St-Sauveur residence, located halfway up one of the numerous wooded mountains in the area.

Standing several hundred feet from the building, the biker had a relatively good view into the forest which spanned below him. To his left, through a clearing in the trees, he could catch a glimpse of the road which wound steeply upwards. A little to his right was a rather deep ravine which pretty much guaranteed that no intruders would arrive from there. Up the slope behind him, the roof of the large country home he was protecting could be seen protruding above the top of the multitude of evergreens which crowded the terrain.

He carefully scanned the woods before him, looking for any signs of activity below; nothing. As he turned his head, carefully scrutinizing the landscape, he sensed, rather than saw, a slight movement by the ravine to his right. Slowly, he crept forward, attempting to make as little noise as possible with the frozen snow underfoot.

As he approached, he felt for the grip of the silenced .22 Beretta Minx tucked in the small of his back. Before he had time to withdraw the weapon, a man's head suddenly appeared over the top of the ravine some fifteen feet away. Initially startled, the man then broke into a smile and finished his climb over the edge.

"Wow, you scared me," the intruder exclaimed, standing and brushing some snow off his black jeans and leather winter jacket.

"This is private property, buddy," Richie warned, remaining alert as the stranger took a couple of steps forward.

The man stopped, giving Richie a puzzled and troubled look before replying.

"Well, yeah. I know. This is Matt's place. I'm Matt's neighbour. I live in the next house down the road. Is there a problem?"

"No. No problem," answered Richie, relaxing a little, not feeling highly threatened by some neighbour maybe twice his age. "Some punks broke into Matt's place so he asked us to keep an eye on it."

"Not too much damage, I hope?" enquired the obviously concerned man as he moved a couple of steps closer.

"Nah, not too much," Richie responded as he leaned against a tree and dug into a pocket for his cigarettes. "Busted some windows and stuff. Nothing serious."

"Well, that's good to hear," the man replied with relief, now standing just a few feet from Richie. "It's getting that we're not safe anywhere anymore. This kind of stuff used to be reserved for the city and now they come out here to rob us."

"Uh, yeah. Right," yawned Richie, becoming bored with this righteous conversation. "Listen. There's gonna be few of us watching the place for a couple of days so it's probably best that you keep off Matt's property for a while. Wouldn't want one of us to take you for a punk, right?"

"Yeah, sure, I understand," the man responded earnestly. "I do some rock climbing and the ravine here is a good spot to practice. But I'll stay out of your way. You be sure to tell Matt to call me if he needs anything. Tommy's the name."

"Sure. I'll do that," Richie chuckled as he turned away to head back to his observation point.

Claude Bouchard

The six inch steel blade plunged through his back into his heart so quickly that he barely had time to feel the pain before dying.

"One down," breathed Chris as he began dragging the dead biker's body the short distance to the ravine.

* * * *

"Good morning! Who's going to Disney World?" asked Gene Fennell as he sat down at the breakfast table.

"We are!" chorused his four kids aged five to ten.

"You bet you are," he beamed proudly at them.

Looking over at his wife who was busy preparing breakfast, he asked, "Bags all ready?"

"Yup," she replied, glancing up at him and flashing a smile. "Once we've got these little monsters fed, we'll be ready to go."

"We've got lots of time," said Gene amidst several anti-monster protests emanating from around the table. "It's only nine o'clock. Flight's at 12:10."

As an inspector for Canada Customs, Gene Fennell had considered that he earned a relatively decent living with his annual salary of $46,268. This, naturally, had excluded the additional perks in the form of contraband merchandise seized from ignorant tourists returning from trips abroad. However, with four kids to raise, a mortgage and two cars, month-ends came quickly and savings, or other luxuries, had not been easy to come by.

This had been the case until Wayne MacKinnon had come along four years ago. Gene had met MacKinnon while carrying out an inspection at Rapid

167

Forwarders, a local customs brokerage operation. They had been introduced by Andy Kovac and the three had ended up going to lunch together. That was when Wayne had put forth his proposal to Gene, outlining the complete drug import scheme to him.

At first, Gene had not believed the man and once he had realized that Wayne was serious, he had been shocked. However, MacKinnon was proposing some serious money for simply overlooking certain shipments of merchandise and Gene had ended up telling Wayne that he would think about it.

That night, he had brought up the subject with his wife who, after a moment of thought, had replied that they didn't open every single parcel, crate or container when they carried out an inspection. Why not just avoid opening those loaded with dope? It was easy money. Money for vacations, stuff for the kids, retirement.

He had contacted Wayne the next morning and suggested the possibility that shipments be identified somehow to ensure that they not be tampered with. This would allow Gene to open only appropriate crates and keep his paper work kosher. Wayne had agreed, thinking that this was a splendid idea, and they were in business.

Gene finished the remains of his coffee and backed away from the kitchen table.

"I'm just gonna hop over to Bill's next door and give him our keys."

Grinning mischievously at his children, still in their seats, he added, "You guys go wash up and go to the bathroom because we're leaving soon. Those who aren't ready are gonna have to stay here."

He laughed as he watched the four of them scramble off. As he started to rise, the front doorbell rang.

'Must be Bill saving me a trip,' he thought, heading for the door and opening it.

Standing on the front porch were two officers of the RCMP.

"Yes? Can I help you?" Gene asked, surprised and puzzled by these unexpected visitors.

"Are you Gene Fennell?" one of the officers asked in a serious tone.

"Y-yeah, yes I am. What seems to be the problem, officer?"

"Mr. Fennell, you are under arrest for conspiring to import illicit narcotics into the country..."

* * * *

Nick Sharp had a reputation of being an honest, experienced cop. The honest part, he had earned over the years by clearly demonstrating that he played by the rules and treated people fairly. The experience had also come with time, time during which he had learned that one couldn't always go by the book 100%. Occasionally, one had to slightly circumvent the system, if only for the sake of expediency.

To this effect, Nick had developed a number of contacts over the years who could discreetly tap a phone line or conveniently turn off someone's electricity for a while. Occasionally, such acts were required urgently and no time was available to get approval through the appropriate channels and, on those occasions, Nick sometimes took advantage of his contacts.

Naturally, Nick never highlighted the fact that such requests were made by the force and no obvious attempt was ever made to use evidence collected by improper means.

On this particular day, considering the schedule that Jonathan had laid out, Nick judged that he had to bend the rules a little. In fact, his intended action was of such a minor nature that he did not even have to consciously decide to make the request.

Picking the phone, he dialled the number of Keith Schmidt, a close friend employed by Bell Mobility, a cellular carrier.

"Keith. How goes it? Fine thanks, but busy as hell. Listen, you got a pen and paper handy? Good. I'm gonna give you a few numbers that should experience technical difficulties real soon. Yeah, three or four hours will be fine. Thanks, bud. I owe you one."

* * * *

Bryan's Mercedes veered wildly into the driveway of Greg's home and came to a screeching halt.

Despite his portly stature, he was up the steps and banging loudly at the door within seconds. Not able to wait for a reply, he headed frantically to one side towards the rear yard, scanning the building for anything unusual.

As he reached the back of the house, his heart sank as he noticed the opened basement door at the far end swaying slightly in the wind. In a frenzy, he hurried over and entered the house, horrified by what he might find but knowing that he had look.

Halfway up the stairs, it dawned on him that if Greg had received a visitor as had Matt, the visitor in question might still be in the building.

Cursing himself for his carelessness, he slowed his pace and pulled out the small pistol he carried in his jacket. He reached the first floor and proceeded hesitantly forward, his heart jumping at every sound.

He prayed that Greg wouldn't be there, that he wouldn't find another massacred corpse as he had at Matt's. He shuddered as he thought of Matt, the image of the battered body covered with burn marks still clearly etched in his brain.

He reached the living room at the front of the house but found it empty. He moved back through the dining room and into the kitchen; still nothing. He glanced into the bathroom as he passed it but everything seemed in order. Continuing down the short hallway, he noticed that the door leading to Greg's study was firmly closed. Grasping the doorknob, he turned it, ever so slowly, until it would turn no more.

After a moment's hesitation, he decided that, if someone was in there, the element of surprise would be more effective than a slow announcement of his arrival. Slamming the door suddenly open, he jumped a step back as he raised his gun in self-defence.

He had nothing to worry about however, for Greg was alone. Alone, slumped in a chair before his computer, his brains splattered on the ceiling, walls and floor of the room. Bryan stared for a moment, as if in a trance, breathing heavily to fight the nausea. In a daze, he returned the gun to his pocket and headed to the front door.

Once into his car, he backed slowly out of the driveway and started his return trip to St-Sauveur, driving carefully, respecting speed limits. He hoped that no neighbours had seen him at Matt's or Greg's. Things were rocky enough as they were.

He suddenly remembered that he was to call Wayne to let him know what he had found. Picking up his cellular phone, he dialled the number to Matt's cottage up north but realized that the phone was no longer working. This was turning out to be a really lousy day.

* * * *

Cathy McCall wandered into the dining room where her husband was reading the morning paper.

"So? Sandy feeling better?" Dave absently asked, glancing up from his reading.

"Couldn't tell you," his wife replied. "There's no answer."

"Therefore, she must be feeling better," he concluded, returning his attention to an article about the never ending saga of Canadian unity.

"I guess," said Cathy doubtfully, unable to shake the strange feeling that something was wrong.

* * * *

Pierre Tardif gathered with the other three plain-clothes RCMP officers at the main entrance of the luxurious condominium complex in Old Montreal.

"There's only one door in the back so you can cover that, Bobby. Jim, once we go in, block the garage door with the car, just in case he tries to use that as an exit. Paul and I will go up and invite the gentleman to join us for a little chat. All set? Let's do this."

As the two others hurried off to their posts, Pierre and Paul entered the large entrance foyer and headed to the doorbell console located to one side. Pierre proceeded to press the buttons of dozen different apartments and stepped back to wait for a response. Within seconds, the intercom started emitting a staticky chorus of, "Hello?, Oui?, Who is it?". However, at least one person responded by pressing the door button, allowing both men access into the building. People were so naive of the security they paid so dearly for.

They headed to the sixth floor and searched the hallway until they found apartment 619. They could hear the faint sounds of a television or radio coming from inside. Pierre knocked on the door as they positioned themselves on either side of it, each with his hand on the grip of his revolver resting in its unsnapped holster.

From within, they heard the sounds of a couple of dead bolts sliding back before the door opened to the extent allowed by the security chain.

"Yes?" asked the attractive blonde through the three inch opening. All she wore was a rather thin silk bathrobe and, although it was just past nine in the morning, Pierre could smell alcohol on her breath.

"Mrs. Sommers?" he enquired, giving her a friendly smile.

"That's right," she confirmed with a faint slur. "What can I do for you?"

"Is Mr. Sommers home?" Pierre politely requested. "We would need to speak to him."

"No, he's at the office," she sneered, pausing to take a solid pull from the glass in her hand. "*Working* with that little whore secretary of his," she added with a sarcastic laugh.

"I see. Sorry to have bothered you, Mrs. Sommers," Pierre apologized.

"Oh, no bother," she responded in a husky voice as she looked him over. "Maybe you want to come in for a drink or, *something?*"

To emphasize the *something*, she shifted her weight a little and raised one knee slightly, exposing quite a lot of firm thigh as a result.

"Ah, as appealing as that invitation sounds, I can't this morning," replied Pierre, flushing, "Maybe some other time."

"Anytime," she replied throatily, licking her lips before closing the door.

* * * *

Blade stood on the west side of Matt's St-Sauveur residence, carefully scanning the hillside above him. It was damn cold but he was tough and could endure anything. After all, he was an Ace of Death.

Quite frankly, he didn't really understand why they were helping these two misfits out; a couple of assholes in suits. But Diamond Jimmy had requested that it be done, so here he was.

Blade was a small man, barely five feet, four inches tall, with an impressive weight of one hundred sixteen pounds, fully clothed. He had grown up in a tough neighbourhood however, where he had been required early on to compensate for his lack of size. By the time he turned thirteen, he had already earned his nickname and it had stuck ever since.

He couldn't see, nor hear anything out of the ordinary in the woods around him. He wondered why he and the other gang members had to freeze out here while the two idiots in suits got to stay inside with that sweet looking dame. Because Diamond Jimmy requested it, he reminded himself once again.

He continued to survey his assigned area, confident that if anybody managed to attack the house behind him, it would not be from this side.

* * * *

"I thought you said we had a lot of work to do?" complained Nancy, her annoyance genuine.

"We do," snickered Allan Sommers, ignoring her tone as he squeezed her buttocks with both hands. "I just think that we need a little break. I have to clear my thoughts."

"But we just got here, Allan," his secretary whined, though she knew that her protests were futile.

"And not a moment too soon," he cooed, sliding one hand under her sweatshirt and fondling her breasts. "Now, why don't you get out of those clothes and have a chat with my friend down here. Come on, baby. You know what I like."

"You're the boss," Nancy sullenly gave in.

She obediently removed her sweatshirt, exposing her delightful twenty-four year old body. As she began to pull down her tight fitting jeans, the door of the office suddenly burst open, startling both she and Sommers.

"Who the fuck are you?" Sommers bellowed angrily, fumbling to re-zip his pants while Nancy scurried behind the desk, trying to hide her half naked body.

"Pierre Tardif, RCMP," the first man informed him, holding out a shield and I.D. card for Sommers' inspection. "This is my partner, Paul Landry."

"Yeah? Well this is a private office, gentlemen," snarled Sommers, "And we're busy right now so you'll have to leave. Call for an appointment on Monday if you need to see me."

"Sorry, Mr. Sommers," insisted Pierre. "No can do. You're under arrest for conspiring to import and distribute illegal narcotics..."

"What? Under arrest? Illegal narcotics?" interrupted Sommers, incredulous. "This is ridiculous."

"Mr. Sommers, you represent a gentleman by the name of James Sanchez, don't you?" asked Pierre. "Otherwise known as Diamond Jimmy?"

"Uh, yes, Mr. Sanchez is one of my clients," responded Sommers uncertainly, taken aback by the question. "But I don't understand what that has to do with your ridiculous accusation of drug trafficking."

"We have a witness who's testified that this office is used for narcotics transactions and storage," Pierre explained.

"This is outrageous," Sommers nervously argued. "This is a law office. Not a goddamn drugstore."

"Listen, Mr. Sommers," Paul Landry spoke soothingly. "We're just doing our job, acting on a tip from a witness. We were told that there was some cocaine stored here right now. Do you mind if we look around? If we don't find anything, that'll take a lot of credibility out of the witness's testimony."

"You want to search this place?" responded Sommers, gaining back some confidence. "Go right ahead. Search the fucking place. You won't find anything. But let me warn you right now. You haven't heard the last of this."

Having received consent, the search began and silence ensued safe for the sounds of Paul Landry opening the drawers and doors of the various pieces of furniture in the room. Within moments he had completed his search and had found nothing.

"What's back there?" he asked, pointing to the door behind Sommers' desk.

"Conference room," snapped Sommers, now fully composed. "Go for it. Search that too. It'll just cost you more when I sue you guys for false arrest, harassment, invasion of privacy and defamation of character."

Paul moved into the conference room and continued his search while the others remained in the main office. After a moment or two, he appeared in the doorway with a strange look on his face. He stared at Sommers as he spoke.

"Would you come in here, Mr. Sommers?"

Sommers rose from his chair, his look of uncertainty having returned, and walked into the conference room.

"Would you like to explain what those are, Mr. Sommers?" Paul demanded, pointing to two bags of white powder on the conference table.

"I-I don't know w-what those are," Sommers stammered. "They're n-not mine. W-where did you find them?"

"In those binders," Paul replied, pointing to two large empty binders, also on the table. "Excellent hiding place, Sommers. I nearly missed them, right there, out in the open in the bookcase."

"So, this whole drug thing is outrageous, Sommers?" challenged Pierre, stepping in. "Then what the hell is this?"

He reached over and picked up the two bags which he tossed at Sommers.

Instinctively catching the bags, the latter pleaded. "These aren't mine. I've been set up. You've got to believe me."

Dazed, he dropped the bags back on the table as Pierre approached and proceeded to handcuff him. "Mr. Sommers, you are under arrest for possession of illegal narcotics."

Sommers' eyes suddenly narrowed as rational thought superseded the shock of the last thirty seconds.

"*You* set me up, you motherfucker," he screamed at Paul Landry. "You brought that shit with you, you bastard."

"Get this guy outta here," ordered Pierre, signalling Bobby and Jim, who stood at the door of the main office.

The two officers escorted the screaming, handcuffed lawyer out of the office and down the hallway towards the bank of elevators. Pierre walked out of the conference room to find the young lady still cowering in the corner behind Sommers' desk. She had since put her clothes back on and appeared extremely frightened.

"What's your name?" he asked gently.

"N-Nancy...Tessier," she replied in a tearful voice.

"O.K., Nancy. Do you know anything about Mr. Sommers being involved in drugs?" Pierre continued.

"N-not really," she stuttered with fear. "I-I n-never saw any drugs but some of h-his clients are g-gang m-members. I s-see their pictures in the p-papers sometimes."

"Don't worry," said Pierre. "You haven't done anything wrong. But we might need you to testify about what happened here today. What did you see?"

"Y-you guys came in and found some drugs in the conference room?" she answered hopefully.

"That's right," Pierre responded, smiling slightly. "Did Mr. Sommers give us permission to search his office?"

"Yes he did," she replied, her expression brightening. "And the conference room."

"Good girl," Pierre nodded. "And Nancy. When we arrived, as far as I'm concerned, you were sitting in a chair writing notes or something while Sommers spoke."

* * * *

From his natural hideout, offered by a series of conifers oddly growing in a circular formation, Jonathan had been observing the guard posted on the west side of the St-Sauveur residence for forty-five minutes. During this time, he was confident that he had established the small man's informal patrolling routine.

After four or five minutes of careful scrutiny from his central watch point at the base of a large oak, the biker would stroll to his right several hundred feet, past where Jonathan sat, nearly to the gravel road which snaked up the incline. He would then return, past his oak tree, walking some four hundred feet to the edge of a deep ravine which horse-shoed around the rear of the property. There, he would scan the portion of the ravine visible to him for several minutes before returning to the foot of the large oak tree to recommence the process.

Satisfied, Jonathan waited for the guard to remake his way to the ravine, absently playing with a length of strong but thin nylon rope in the interim. Within a few minutes, it was time and he quickly and stealthily made his way to his chosen point of attack; the large oak tree.

Blade returned from the ravine and settled once again at the foot of the big tree. He was getting bored and cold. He wished the stupid fucks inside would bring him a cup of coffee or something. After all, he was protecting them. The least the bastards could do was show a little consideration. God, it was cold.

He wondered if the cold would bother him less if he was stoned and decided to find out. Anyways, nothing was going on, and if something did happen, it wasn't the fact that he'd have smoked a joint that would change anything. A good old THC buzz actually sharpened one's senses, he had always believed.

He pulled a joint from his cigarette pack and lit it, sucking the heavy smoke deeply into his lungs and holding it for several seconds before exhaling. He smiled, already feeling the effect after one toke. It was grass, Thai, but its quality and potency surpassed that of any hash he'd ever done, even Kashmir or black Columbian. He pulled in another lungful of the wonderful smoke, holding his breath until he'd counted to thirty. He chuckled to himself and leaned his back against the large tree, content. Getting stoned, he decided, definitely helped ward off the cold. He took another hefty toke and chuckled again.

Several feet above Blade's head, the trunk of the mammoth oak tree branched off rather symmetrically into four massive limbs. Sometime in the past, a prior owner of Matt's property had begun building a tree house, using the four large branches as the natural foundation for the structure. For reasons unknown, construction had ceased once the floor had been completed, rendering the tree house into simply an observation platform, some eight feet off the ground. It might not have served much purpose in the past, but on this day, Jonathan thanked its builder, whoever and wherever he was. For today, the platform, on which Jonathan was now perched, was a gift from heaven. Its existence almost made the task at hand too easy.

Below him, the small man had lit a joint a few minutes earlier and, judging from his almost continuous, quiet chuckling, was obviously quite stoned; another gift from heaven.

Ever so slowly, Jonathan raised himself to a kneeling position, praying for the old grey boards not to creak. They didn't. The Lord was generous today. He inched to the edge of the platform and soon could see the small man, his head, just a few feet away.

His rope ready, he tossed the noose quickly, expertly, landing it perfectly around his target's head. With a forceful, upward yank, he jerked the small biker's body a couple of feet off the ground. Although he'd heard the unmistakable crack of the neck snapping, he held on, keeping the body suspended until it stopped twitching. He then lowered it slowly, intent on avoiding to make any unnecessary noise.

After descending from the tree and ensuring that the guard was in fact dead, he picked up the body and hurried quietly through the woods, away from the house. Several hundred yards further, a cluster of pine trees supplied appropriate cover for the corpse.

He dumped the body and returned towards the house, erasing his tracks as he went. He hoped Chris was getting along as well as he was.

* * * *

Thai Airlines' Flight 835 in from Hong Kong landed right on schedule at Phuket International Airport; 8:17 p.m., local time.

The variety of tourists disembarked from the 747 onto the runway and climbed into the bus which would drive them to the airport terminal, a walking distance away. Hans Fritz had been here often in the past and had always found amusing, this bus ride which lasted all of thirty seconds. His theory was that the airport authorities had purchased the bus in haste when the airport had been built and were too proud to admit their error. Therefore, any traveller arriving was required to board the bus for a half minute trip, a process which sometimes took as much as fifteen minutes from start to finish.

Hans had remained close to the door inside the bus and was one of the first to go through customs and immigration.

"Passport and declaration, please," barked the stout customs officer with the mock sternness such public servants display worldwide.

Without a word, Hans complied with the man's request.

"The purpose of your trip, Mr. Fritz?" demanded the man as he examined the passport.

"Mostly business, I'm afraid," replied Hans with a warm smile. "I am here to help export some more of your lovely pearls."

"You are staying how long?"

"Only two days, unfortunately," answered Hans, his tone one of disappointment.

"Please try to visit our beaches," suggested the officer, dropping the tough facade. "Have a nice stay."

"Thank-you. And I will try to visit your lovely beaches but, as they say, business before pleasure."

He strolled into the small terminal, searching for a familiar face and they saw each other at the same time. Neither had ever met before but they had each been faxed photos of the other and they knew of each other's reputation through the grapevine.

"Mister Fritz, I presume," she said as she approached with an extended hand.

The photograph had not done her justice. To say she was gorgeous would have been an understatement.

"Miss Tahashi, a pleasure," he replied, taking her small but firm hand in his and shaking it warmly.

"Call me Kim, please. And I will call you Hans," she proposed, flashing a heavenly smile. "Come. I have a Jeep waiting outside."

They left the terminal in silence, each evaluating their first impression of the other. Once settled into the Jeep with Kim at the wheel, they headed south on highway 402.

"So, you are the famous Jeweller," stated Kim, concentrating on the narrow winding road.

"Infamous, perhaps," Hans chuckled. "And you are the famous Teacher. What brings a Japanese English teacher to Phuket?"

"I was actually here for a week of vacation when I received the call," she replied. "I had flown in from Tokyo last night. How long will you be here?"

"A couple of days only," he sighed. "I was due to make a trip shortly to visit some suppliers so it will be done. You're staying at Le Méridien?"

"Yes I am. And you?"

"The same," he said. "Perhaps once we're done, I could have the honour of buying you dinner?"

She smiled before replying. "I have already reserved a lagoon-side table at Pakarang for 10:30. I trust that that gives us sufficient time?"

He looked at his watch which read 8:47. "Yes, my dear. More than enough time."

* * * *

"I'm worried about Sandy and Chris," Cathy stated, interrupting her husband's reading once again. "I call and there's no answer. When I try their cell phones, I get the message service."

"They could be gone shopping, skiing, you name it," Dave replied, a touch of exasperation in his voice. "Honey, what's the matter with you? So what, they're not home? You know Chris and Sandy. They're always on the go."

"Sandy never called me back yesterday," retorted his wife, her tone equally impatient. "That's not like her. Don't believe me if you don't want to but something is wrong, Dave."

"Cathy?" he called as she stormed out of the dining room.

Receiving no response, he shrugged and returned his attention to his newspaper. One thing was certain. She would not disturb his reading for a little while.

* * * *

The building had existed on the outskirts of Phuket City for about ten years. One hundred feet wide and about sixty deep, it housed the operations of a clothing manufacturer and employed seventy-five locals who worked for the pittance wages often customary in many Asian countries. T-shirts and other sportswear were the major product lines, mostly produced for export to Europe and the Americas.

Although the operation was profitable, in recent years it had become a cover for a much more lucrative business. For within the two-storey building's high barn-like roof was probably Asia's most highly advanced heroin refining laboratory. Few people were aware of its existence as access to this part of the structure was well concealed and the lab itself was perfectly sound-proofed.

On evenings and weekends, a guard was posted at both the front and back of the building as an extra precaution. Vandalism and theft did occur occasionally in the area, so the presence of these individuals was not viewed as uncommon by the odd passer-by. Most watch-shifts however, were uneventful, leaving the guards with little to experience barring boredom.

Unfortunately, this would not be the case for the two men on duty on this particular evening.

Prasop really did not enjoy working on the Saturday night shift. Although the job was never exciting on any given night, having to be there on Saturdays was frustrating in addition to being boring. Saturdays were, after all, party nights when the young ladies went into the bars and loosened up. But a job was a job and more importantly, the boss was the boss. He also had to consider that this particular employment allowed him access to the 24 Hours Bar, where the tough guys socialized. This gave him special status which served to impress the majority of available young ladies.

As he sat on the old wooden crate which served as his chair, he heard a dull thud come from his right. Standing up, he took several steps in the dirt parking area which spanned the rear of the building. Searching the darkness, he saw nothing. He started to turn back when another similar sound occurred. Turning sharply towards the noise, he withdrew his revolver and moved cautiously forward, peering into the night. Another thud came, a little more to the left this time, the sound of a stone hitting the packed earth.

He continued to advance, slowly, searching the night in vain. Another one, this time to his right. Adrenalin pumping, he moved quickly in that direction, advancing a dozen yards before stopping to listen. Motionless, he stood there, straining to hear anything out of the ordinary. Nothing. He scanned the area, turning slowly until he had completed a full circle. Still nothing. He remained in this spot for several minutes, continuing to circle, searching for the cause of the unusual disturbance, completely unaware that this would be his last Saturday night.

Past the parking area behind the building was a ditch, overgrown with a variety of weeds, brush and shrubs. It offered excellent cover although Ron Singer hoped none of it was vegetation of a poisonous kind.

Upon his arrival, he had been disappointed to see the guard seated on a wooden box, his back leaned against the wall of the structure. With no cover close by, the element of surprise became non-existent. As time had gone by, his disappointment had grown as he realized that the man did not even leave his post to patrol the area. Ron had come to the conclusion that he would have to draw the guard out if he wanted to settle this assignment that night.

Banking on the hope that the guard was not too bright, he found several stones, large enough to create an audible sound upon landing. These, he proceeded to toss, one by one, to attract the other man's attention. By the fourth stone, the guard stood less than fifteen feet away, frantically searching for the source of the noises. After several minutes, he seemed to relax and decided to head back to the comfort of his wooden crate.

Only seconds were required for Ron, an expert in this type of activity, to silently cross the short span separating them. The garrotte swung swiftly, perfectly around the Asian's neck, his death, almost instantaneous.

Ron dumped the body into the ditch and headed towards the front of the building to see if his brother Mike needed any assistance.

* * * *

Arnie Schwartz had always looked for ways to make an easy buck. He was generally lazy and thus, strongly believed in the concept of getting as much as possible for the least effort. He didn't hide this fact and often boasted that this was the main reason why he had gone to work for the government. Decent gains for little effort.

He particularly enjoyed working as a customs officer, not for the job itself but rather, for the side benefits it offered if one was smart enough to take advantage of them. Loads of seized merchandise were poorly accounted for and there for the taking. So Arnie took, a lot, for personal consumption as well as for sale to others.

Eighteen months ago, he had been enraged to learn that he was being transferred to warehouse inspection duty. Recognizing that such a transfer would put an end to his profitable secondary business, he had argued with his supervisor but, to no avail. It was transfer or leave, due to personnel reductions.

Grudgingly, he had transferred to warehouse inspections, where he had begun his new duties; inspecting random commercial shipments imported into the country. The job wasn't bad, definitely not tiring, although Arnie saw little possibility of maintaining his sideline. At least, his partner, Gene Fennell, was a good guy who liked to listen to Arnie's anecdotes about long-term borrowing of seized merchandise.

At the end of his second week in his new position, he was having lunch with Gene, when the latter proposed an opportunity to Arnie which made his former sideline seem like pocket change. Arnie had willingly agreed to participate in Gene's 'narcotics overlooking' activities and had been financially content ever since.

The shrill shrieking of the phone amplified the ringing in his head. He had suspected that he would suffer from a hangover in the morning but had not expected anything like this. He rolled over, hiding his face from the light with a pillow as he desperately grasped for the phone.

"Yeah?" he groaned, hoping to hell it was an emergency.

"Arnie?" a woman's voice cried. "They came to get Gene, Arnie! You've gotta help!"

"What the fuck?" Arnie muttered, confused as he sat up in bed. "Who is this? What the hell is going on?"

"This is Lisa Fennell, Arnie. Gene's wife," the shaky voice replied. "About forty-five minutes ago, they came to get Gene. I've been looking for your number everywhere. You've got to help, Arnie. Please!"

Gene? Lisa Fennell? Gene Fennell. His partner. He was starting to understand. A little.

"O.K. Lisa. Calm down. Who came to get Gene? What's going on?"

"The police, Arnie," Lisa sobbed, breaking down again. "It said RCMP on their jackets and on the cars. You've got to help, Arnie. They arrested Gene.

Because of the drugs. We were going on vacation. They took him away. Please!"

"Take it easy, Lisa," ordered Arnie, no longer concerned with his hangover. "Arnie will take care of everything. Just relax. I'm gonna hang up now cuz I have some calls to make. Don't worry. I'm gonna fix this, O.K.? Now, don't call me back cuz I don't want to tie up the phone. I'll let you know what's going on. Don't worry."

With that, he slammed down the phone and scrambled to get some clothes on. As he hurriedly tied his shirt, he peered through the partially opened vertical blinds to the street below. Nothing. But he had to hurry. If they knew about Gene, they knew about him. Or, they would soon.

He praised himself for his silly habit of keeping cash handy. Rushing into the storage closet of his second storey condo, he pulled out his stash and counted; $4,700. That would cover him for several days. He'd make some withdrawals from cash machines but he'd have to be careful. The cops would trace that. Credit cards would be iffy too. At least he had something to start with. Now, the priority however, was to leave. The cops could show up any second.

Running into the entrance hall, he jammed his feet into his untied running shoes as he frantically pulled his ski jacket from the closet. He bolted from his apartment, not bothering to close the door behind him and headed for the parking garage, two levels below.

RCMP detectives Eric Levesque and Daniel Samson were approaching the Belanger Street building in Anjou where Arnie Schwartz resided when a candy apple red Mustang GT roared out of the inside parking, swerving wildly to avoid colliding with their vehicle.

"That's him, Eric," Daniel exclaimed. "Red Mustang GT. That's Schwartz. Go!"

Levesque threw the gear shift of their Taurus in reverse and backed out of the entrance with tires screaming. Down the hill, they could see Schwartz's vehicle turn right on the red at Langelier, narrowly missing an approaching pickup truck.

"He's going for the Met," predicted Samson, referring to the Metropolitan, Montreal's elevated throughway.

With sirens blaring, they took pursuit of the red Mustang, both vehicles running through three other red lights before engaging onto the westbound Met.

Here, Schwartz opened up the powerful engine of his automobile, quickly increasing his speed to ninety miles per hour as he dodged in and out of the Saturday morning traffic.

"We're not gonna have to catch this guy," muttered Levesque as he hesitantly increased his speed on the icy road. "He's gonna kill himself."

As if his words were a command, the Mustang suddenly went out of control as it swerved to avoid a car coming up an on-ramp ahead. Recent heavy snow, followed by a sudden drop in temperatures had turned the sides of the elevated highway into dangerous jump ramps. Several cars had already gone off the road in the last week.

The Mustang spun two perfect three-sixties before projecting itself a dozen feet above the level of the road where, for a fraction of a second, it seemed to hang in mid-air. Then gravity took effect, violently pulling the car to its smashing end, twenty-five feet below.

Several minutes were required for Levesque and Samson to make it down to the site of the crash. By the time they got there, a crowd had formed and an ambulance was already on the scene. The driver of the Mustang, the detectives were informed, had died on impact.

* * * *

The road which ran in front of the clothing manufacture and into Phuket City dropped into a steep hill a quarter mile past the building. Mike and Ron Singer had parked their vehicles at the bottom of this incline and proceeded on foot, Ron heading for the rear of the structure while Mike cut through the field across the road.

After ten minutes of hiking through the tall weeds, he had found himself directly ahead of the building, a hundred yards away. Here, he had settled comfortably and begun observing the rather mundane activities of his eventual victim.

Looking at his watch, he acknowledged that it was time to go and began retracing his steps towards the vehicles. Once hidden by the top of the incline, he cut across to the road and turned back towards the building. As he reached the top of the hill, he slowed his pace, incorporating a slight irregular stagger to his walk as he headed towards the guard.

Tridhosyuth tensed a little as he watched the figure approaching in the darkness. Although the man was alone, he seemed to be speaking, mumbling to himself. Every once in a while he walked slightly out of step as if unsure of his balance.

"Crazy drunk tourist," Tridhosyuth cursed under his breath, rising to his feet.

"Hello, there," the foreigner called out, his accent unmistakably American. "Do you speak English?"

"A little," the guard responded. "This private area. You go away."

"Sure, sure," the American slurred, stopping in his tracks and holding up both hands. "I ain't looking for trouble. I'm just a bit lost."

"Where you go?" asked Tridhosyuth, willing to help the drunk leave.

"Well, a bunch of us took a little bus from the hotel to town, ya know," the man explained, wavering slightly. "We had a few drinks in a bar and I went out to get some air, ya know. Started walking but I sorta lost my bearings."

"Town? Phuket City?" asked the guard, confused by the American's language. "You go there?"

"Yeah, Phuket City," laughed the drunk, take a few steps forward. "Downtown, ya know, where I can take the bus."

"Phuket City, downtown, that way," answered Tridhosyuth, pointing in the direction from which the drunk had come.

"Well, goddamn, I was headed the wrong way," the drunk guffawed, totally amused by the situation. "Thanks a bunch. You're a good man."

As the guard returned to his seat, the American turned away and staggered a few steps, stopped and turned back again.

"Oh, by the way," he said, the drunken slur gone. "Thanks for letting me get so close."

With expert precision, he fired the silenced handgun which he inconspicuously produced, hitting Tridhosyuth twice in the forehead and once in the heart.

"You've made my job so much easier."

* * * *

192

From a small natural shelf four feet below the edge of the ravine, Chris had been watching the guard at the back of the St-Sauveur chalet for the better part of a half hour.

This one might prove to be difficult. For one, there was little cover near the man, making a surprise attack unfeasible. The lack of cover also made the guard and the surrounding area much more visible from the house, should anyone decide to glance outside. Chris' biggest concern however, was the man's sheer size; at least six-four and probably close to three hundred pounds. Thoughts of a possible one on one combat with this gorilla made him shudder.

The guard started one of his patrol walks again, as he had done a half dozen times so far. Chris pressed himself into the recess under the edge of the ravine, once again holding his breath and covering his nose and mouth, lest the steam of his breath give him away. Above his head, the giant's boots crunched past in the snow. Chris waited, still not clear on how he would eliminate the man.

* * * *

A few minutes before reaching Patong Beach, Hans climbed into the back of the mini-van and, reaching under the seat, pulled out the twenty inch long case which had formed the bottom of his carry-on bag. Opening the case, he quickly assembled the various components and was ready in no time.

"How do you get that through the airports?" Kim asked curiously from the driver's seat as she watched him in the rear-view mirror.

"Most of it's plastic," Hans proudly replied. "I made it myself. A talent I've acquired over the years."

"Plastic?" Kim exclaimed, intrigued. "Won't it melt?"

"Yes," Hans grinned. "Single use only. Sort of like those disposable tourist cameras."

"What about the shell?" persisted a curious Kim.

"I make those too. They look like a can of deodorant, even on close examination. I carry them in my suitcase."

They ceased their conversation and both donned nylon stocking masks as they rolled onto the main strip of Patong Beach. Kim slowed the vehicle and pulled onto the left side of the road, stopping directly in front a short side street lined with a half dozen bars on either side. At the end of the street, directly facing them, was the 24 Hours Bar.

Known and avoided by the locals as a fraternizing spot for the tougher crowd, it was actually an exclusive club for a group of organized criminals specializing in the refining and subsequent exporting of heroin.

With the mini-van barely stopped, Hans pulled open the sliding side door and climbed out, weapon in hand. He took several steps forward as he raised the cylindrical shaped object to his shoulder, paying no attention to the awed onlookers. Coming to a halt, he dropped to one knee, looked through the sight and, following a slight pause to ensure proper aim, pulled the trigger.

With a roaring whoosh, the rocket seared down the street and through the open doors of the 24 Hours Bar. A fraction of a second, which seemed like an hour, went by with no result. Then, as if by magic, the building seemed to expand as it exploded into flame, leaving none of its occupants as survivors.

Hans smiled at the shocked witnesses through his nylon mask, waving as he quickly, yet casually strolled back and climbed into the already moving mini-van.

"That went well," commented Kim, pulling off her mask as they sped out of the village.

"Indeed it did," agreed Hans, looking at his watch. "I do believe we'll have time to dump this van *and* have a drink at the bar before dinner."

* * * *

In frustration, Jonathan observed the guard on the wide front porch of Matt's Laurentian hideaway. In forty minutes, the man had left the porch once, to saunter down the driveway to the road; only once. No checking the woods on either side, no quick walks along the road to search for suspicious vehicles. He just stood on the damn porch.

After careful consideration, Jonathan made up his mind. He would have to get a hold of Chris before attempting to get rid of this guard. Between the two of them, they'd have a better chance. Silently, he made his way among the trees towards the back of the house.

* * * *

Followed by a Jeep, the small closed-box pickup truck rolled into the parking area behind the building, coming to a stop before the large shipping/receiving door. Ron Singer climbed out and, with the help of a set of industrial metal cutters, snipped the two heavy padlocks which secured this entrance. After opening the door, he returned to the truck and drove it into the building, parking it in the center of the empty shipping area. He hurried out, closing the large door behind him before joining his brother in the Jeep and they drove off in the direction of Phuket City, their task nearly complete.

After a couple of minutes, Ron pulled a small remote control device from his pocket, much like those used to activate car alarms. He calmly pressed a button and returned the object to his pocket. From a few miles behind them came a huge orange glow, immediately followed by a deep rumbling which could be both felt and heard.

Their task was complete.

* * * *

Bull, due to his size and appearance, was generally presumed to be a rather unintelligent individual. As many had unfortunately learned over the years however, he wasn't completely stupid.

He had caught a glimpse of the man hiding on the edge of the ravine almost twenty minutes earlier. He knew that the intruder had not been there very long because he had looked down into the ravine along the length of his watch area as little as fifteen minutes before spotting the man.

He hadn't made any moves yet, believing that time could an excellent ally. When one played it one's way, a little time could conveniently lull an adversary into a false sense of security. But as Bull returned from the east side of the house, he decided that his adversary must be sufficiently lulled.

"Don't make any sudden moves, Mister," he ordered in a surprisingly soft voice. "Or I'll blow your fucking brains out."

Considering the barrel of the shotgun aimed at his head from some six inches away, Chris felt compelled to comply with the man's request.

"Get up here. Now."

Chris climbed over the edge as the ape backed away a couple of feet.

"Listen, I don't know what the problem is and I'm not looking for any trouble. I'm just rock climbing. That's all."

"Yeah?" sneered Bull. "Why you been sitting on the ledge for twenty minutes watching me?"

"W-well," Chris stammered, his mind racing.

The bastard had known he was there.

"W-when I saw you with the gun, I got scared. I-I didn't want to make any noise and end up getting shot. Come on. I live in the house down the hill. I practice climbing here all the time. Matt doesn't mind."

"What's your name, Mister?" asked the giant, apparently brighter than his counterpart whom Chris had met earlier.

"Paul. Paul Wessell," Chris replied convincingly.

"O.K. Paul," Bull said with an unfriendly smile. "Show me some I.D. Show me something with the name Paul Wessell on it and I'll let you go home."

"I-I don't have my wallet with me," argued Chris, starting to really worry. "I was out climbing in my backyard, for Chrissakes."

Bull tightened his grip slightly on the shotgun as he spoke. "Empty your pockets, Mister. Real slow. Cuz I don't think you're no Paul Wessell. I think you may be the bastard these fuckers inside are scared of."

Speechless, Chris stared at the ape and started to tremble. Slowly, he reached into a side pocket of his jacket and pulled out his wallet. As he held it out to Bull, it dropped from his badly shaking hand.

"Thought you had no wallet, Paul?" Bull chided. "Pick it up."

'Thank-you,' Chris thought as he crouched down, bending forward towards the wallet.

With sudden force, he lunged forward, closing the short distance which separated them. His left shoulder smashed into the huge man's stomach, just below the rib cage, causing an audible cracking sound. Reaching up into the air, he grabbed desperately for the guard's gun and, miraculously, found his hand wrapping around the cold steel of the double barrel. He jerked violently, sending the rifle flying high and then clattering down into the ravine.

At that moment, he felt the gorilla's hands reach under his armpits and straighten him back to a standing position, as does a child with a rag doll. He stared into the giant's eyes and could see that he had caused him pain. Unfortunately, it had been too little pain; much, much too little.

The hands quickly slid from his armpits to his neck and suddenly, his feet were no longer touching the ground. He kicked the ape in the ribs as the latter held him suspended by the throat. The kicks seemed to have little effect safe for encouraging the giant to squeeze Chris's neck a little harder. He could no longer breathe and was starting to lose consciousness.

'I love you, Sandy,' he thought sadly, realizing that he was about to die and would never see her again.

His vision was growing extremely hazy and he was starting to hallucinate. It was like watching a movie in which he had a central role. He could see his feet dangling above the ground, the gorilla's angry smiling face, Jonathan behind them pointing a gun. It was all so dreamlike.

He crashed to ground suddenly and was aware of severe pain as something extremely heavy fell on top of him. He was confused and his neck hurt really badly, but he could breathe. The pressure was gone from his throat, he was lying on the ground under some dead-weight and he could breathe.

"Come on, Chris," Jonathan's voice whispered hoarsely in his ear. "We gotta get out of here. Anybody looks out those windows, it's all over."

With the added luxury of oxygen, Chris's thought process was returning back to normal at a rapid pace. He sat up, pushing the ape's body off him as Jonathan pulled. Definitely not less than three hundred pounds.

Two holes were clearly visible on the left side of the man's head. The other side, where the bullets had exited, was a mess. They rolled the heavy body a few feet and watched it tumble and slide down the side of the deep ravine, then hurried off for the cover of the woods, waiting to be clearly out of sight and earshot before speaking.

"Thanks," rasped Chris, massaging his bruised neck.

"All in a day's work," replied Jonathan with a quick smile as he replaced the two missing bullets in his silenced pistol's magazine. "One to go."

* * * *

Along the north shore of Laval spanned Mille-Iles Boulevard, named after the river which stretched the length of that side of the island. The area near Autoroute 25, in the eastern part of Laval, was sparsely developed residentially, home mostly to farms and woods.

If one drove along Mille-Iles Boulevard, east of the 25, one eventually saw a large fenced-in area located between the road and the river. Barbed wire lined the top of the fence and surveillance cameras were visible around the property. Seated several hundred feet from the road was a large two storey residential structure which was regularly patrolled by guards clad in blue jeans and leather jackets. This was the headquarters of the Aces of Death and the home of Diamond Jimmy Sanchez.

As is the case with most such gangs, the Aces of Death made little effort to hide who they were or what they did. What the public, and even police, knew was not a problem. The main thing was to ensure that nothing could be proven in a court of law. Keeping at least one step ahead of justice was the name of the game.

This was a concept that Diamond Jimmy was well aware of and he had built his residence accordingly. Very few trees or any other type of cover could be found on the grounds. Motion sensors were strategically hidden all over the property and pressure detectors, able to detect any weight in excess of twenty-five pounds, had been systematically buried under the vast lawns. From dusk till dawn, powerful halogen spots washed the entire property in their harsh light. Naturally, the house itself was equipped with a security system rivalling that of the Royal Canadian Mint and, at any given time of the day or night, the surveillance centre was manned by no less than four highly trained technicians.

No surprise attacks or ambushes from other gangs, nor raids from the cops would take place here without the headquarters' occupants being well aware.

This, of course, was information that was known by the police, which allowed Nick Sharp to plan the RCMP visit to Diamond Jimmy's fortress accordingly.

Since this was a major operation which would surely become public knowledge, it was to be played strictly by the book. By 8:30, Nick's file preparation specialists, with the help of Greg's journal and other data which Jonathan had supplied, had put together a sufficiently convincing dossier of 'past' surveillance operations and informant evidence for Nick to officially use. With it, he quickly obtained the required authorization to set his plan in motion, which included cutting power, phone service, water supply and gas. The operation, scheduled for ten o'clock, would also require an army of some fifty officers.

Claude Bouchard

Today, they would bring down Diamond Jimmy and the Aces of Death.

* * * *

The rented helicopter left the airport at Bucaramanga and headed southwest, into the mountains towards Málaga. At the stick was Wild Billy Harrelson, ace chopper pilot and a veteran from the Vietnam War.

Contrary to many of his peers from Nam, Billy had not returned angry at the government or suffering from post-traumatic stress disorder, although he would have had every reason to do so. He had not agreed with the war and had lost his right leg fighting it. However, the army had taught him how to fly a chopper and Vietnam had given him the opportunity to really learn how to maneuver such a machine.

Upon his return and following his convalescence, he had started a helicopter ride business in Hawaii, offering the ultimate thrill to the ultimate thrill-seeker.

He also did some 'consulting' work on the side. Today was a consulting assignment.

Seated next to Billy was Freddy "Guns" Mager, also a Nam veteran and long time friend. Freddy was the one who had introduced Billy to the 'consulting' a few years earlier, a career which he himself had embarked in immediately after the war. Three or four assignments a year were sufficient to keep him overly comfortable financially, allowing him much leisure time which he spent travelling the world on "Victory", his sixty foot yacht.

Neither man was worried about today's mission. They had both been involved in others, much more complex.

201

As Freddy often said, "Every once in a while, they throw in an easy one. Ya know, bonus money."

* * * *

At precisely 10 o'clock, all utilities were cut to the headquarters of the Aces of Death. At the same time, a heavily armoured tractor trailer smashed through the main gate at break-neck speed and rushed towards the building. As it veered sideways in front of the house and screeched to a halt, side panels on the trailer slid open, letting out dozens of officers in full protective gear.

In the meantime, a second identical vehicle was also emptying its cargo of manpower, these men quickly taking position around the perimeter of the property outside the fence.

Inside the house, Diamond Jimmy was in a basement room, commonly referred to as the "lab", with a couple of subordinates. This room was generally used to test, cut, weigh and repackage narcotics, hence its name.

Having chemically tested the coke for its purity and composition, Jimmy was sitting at a glass covered table, preparing a line for a "physical" test. As he leaned forward to snort the white powder, the windowless room went completely dark.

"What the fuck?" he bellowed as the battery-powered emergency lights came on, filling the room with an eerie glow. "Goddamn fucking Hydro."

Several seconds later, the power returned, accompanied by the low distant rumble of the large gasoline powered generator located in the garage. At that moment, the door of the room burst open and one of his guards on duty rushed in.

"Jimmy, we've got a fucking problem," he breathlessly exclaimed. "A fucking raid. They got two trucks full of cops surrounding the goddamn place. They busted through the front gate. They got a fucking army."

"Jesus Christ," screamed Jimmy in frustration.

He turned to the two in the lab. "Dump the shit. Burn it. Now."

He hurried out of the lab while the two started loading the bags of coke in the high intensity gas incinerator foreseen for just such an occasion. He preferred to lose eighteen kilos of cocaine than spend an equivalent number of years in jail.

Unfortunately, when the power had gone out, the gas had been cut as well.

* * * *

"We'll be there in about five minutes," shouted Wild Billy over the roar of the chopper's engine.

Guns Mager nodded and climbed into the open cargo space in the back to set up his equipment.

As one might guess, Guns had earned his nickname due to his passion for firearms of all kinds. As a child, he had started by making his own slingshots and by the age of seven, had easily convinced his father, a hunting fanatic, to buy him a pellet rifle. He'd gone on his first hunting trip at eight and by the time he'd turned ten, he was already known as *the* gun expert in his county.

Not only was he an exceptional shot, he was also a walking encyclopaedia on any and all subjects related to firearms, big or small. He started designing and building his own guns before becoming a teenager, a hobby which he had maintained and perfected since.

The weapon of the day was one of his creations and its functioning was actually quite simple. In fact, it was actually a large scale model of a compressed gas pellet gun; very large scale. A three foot length of two and a half inch pipe served as the barrel which was mounted on a five pound canister of compressed carbon dioxide. Appropriately modified hand grenades replaced the pellets and six could be loaded in the ammunition dispenser at a time. Pulling the trigger released a sudden measured burst of gas into the barrel which projected the grenade.

It was accurate to one hundred feet and with Wild Billy as his pilot, Guns knew that they'd come in much closer than that.

* * * *

"This is the RCMP," Nick Sharp's voice echoed metallically through the bullhorn in the cold morning air. "We have the property surrounded. We have a warrant to search the premises. If we're not granted access, we will use force to enter the building."

Lowering the bullhorn, he turned to François Duguay, Regional Commander of the Quebec Provincial Police. "We'll give them a minute to respond. If they don't open up, we break in."

* * * *

"You got that shit burning?" demanded Jimmy as he rushed back into the lab.

204

"Yeah, just started," replied his subordinate. "Fuckers cut the gas too. Had to use the backup tanks."

"Bastards," hissed Jimmy, staring at the incinerator as it turned a fortune of coke into nothing. "We have nothing else in here?"

"Nope," assured his lackey. "They'll find a few guns but that's it."

"Fucking waste of taxpayers' money," Jimmy muttered. "I'm gonna make these cocksuckers pay someday."

* * * *

The helicopter came over the last ridge and their target was in sight. Two buildings; a barn, which was really the cocaine processing lab, and an old farmhouse used for sleeping and eating. Behind these structures was a small landing strip for the planes that flew the coke out of the area. A half dozen Jeeps and pickup trucks were parked haphazardly around the buildings, indicating that several people were on the premises. A lone guard, armed with an automatic weapon, rose from his seat by the barn entrance as the helicopter approached.

Playing with the throttle, Billy started sporadically increasing and decreasing the revolutions of the engine. This, combined with the erratic swaying of the chopper, left a clear impression that the machine was experiencing mechanical problems.

As they came down into the clearing before the buildings, Billy waved the guard frantically back, and the latter seemed more than happy to comply.

With the helicopter no more than a half dozen feet from the ground, Billy suddenly swung the machine sideways, exposing the open cargo door.

Mager fired off three rapid shots with a handgun, hitting the guard on all counts.

Dropping the pistol, he turned his attention to his grenade launcher, taking aim at a window of the barn. He pulled the trigger four times, proudly observing each of his projectiles make their way into the old wooden building. After all, it was barely thirty feet away.

The chopper swung 90 degrees and Guns expertly delivered the two remaining grenades through a window of the farmhouse.

Billy opened the throttle and the helicopter quickly rose as it turned before speeding off back over the nearby hills, leaving a series of massive explosions in the background.

From start to finish, the operation had taken twenty-three seconds.

"See? What'd I tell ya?" shouted a grinning Guns as he climbed back into the front seat. "Bonus money."

* * * *

"Chief," called out the officer as he ran over to Nick Sharp and François Duguay.

"They've got a fire going," he said, pointing towards the roof of the building.

Looking up, they could see the heat haze accompanied by light smoke shooting out of a chimney.

"Bastards are burning their stash," Nick commented with a smile.

"Poor Jimmy," replied François. "This is really gonna turn out to be a lousy day for him."

Nick nodded as he raised the bullhorn to his lips.

"This is your last chance. Open the door or we will come in by force."

He waited a few seconds, then nodded to an officer already seated in a small but powerful armoured tractor which had been lifted out of the trailer. The diesel engine rumbled and the machine began rolling forward, its pointed, plough-like front aimed at the main door of the house. A dozen officers quickly fell in formation behind it.

With the tractor no more than ten feet from its target, the door suddenly opened and a voice called out from within.

"O.K. We ain't looking for no trouble. You guys want to come in and fuck up our morning, go ahead."

Through the bullhorn, Nick replied, "I want everybody in the house to assemble in the living room, arms spread, up against the walls. You have one minute. Then we're coming in."

He signalled his officers who quickly approached the building, lining up along its walls on either side of the entrance.

"At least they're cooperating," François murmured approvingly.

Nick turned to him and with a grim smile said, "My friend, don't trust these fuckers for a second. If you do, you're dead. Let's go."

They walked to the front door, preceded by a dozen officers with weapons drawn, and entered the large house.

The living room, to the left, was surprisingly well decorated. Apparently Diamond Jimmy insisted on comfort. As requested, the occupants, fourteen in all, were lined along the walls, although none had assumed the desired position.

"All right, gentlemen," Nick addressed the group. "You know the routine. You've all been there before. Hands against the wall and spread em."

With a lazy nonchalance, all but one of the gang members complied, some chuckling, others exaggerating the requested spread-eagled stance.

The non-complier approached a step with hands spread. He was Shaun "Chains" Wilson, the undisputed second-in-command of the Aces of Death.

He stared coolly at Nick as he spoke.

"Before we go any further, I'd like to know who the fuck you are and I wanna see your fucking warrant."

Nick eyed Chains for a moment, then walked up to him until their faces were a half inch apart.

"I'm RCMP Chief Nicholas Sharp, you little piece of shit. Now get yourself against the wall real quick or I'll blow your fucking brains out."

He leaned the barrel of his withdrawn Colt .45 against Chains' right temple as added incentive. Following a fiery ten second stare, the gang member stepped back and slowly moved to the wall. Nick gestured and a number of his officers began frisking the bikers while others went off to explore the rest of the house. Quickly, the pile of compulsory switchblades grew in the middle of the carpeted floor.

Scanning their prisoners, Nick's stomach tightened as he realized that his main objective was not present.

"Where's Jimmy Sanchez?" he demanded.

In response, Jimmy strutted in from the next room, apparently having been simply waiting for his cue.

"Howya doin, Nicky-boy?" he smirked as he dropped on a nearby sofa.

"Up against the wall, Sanchez," Nick ordered.

"Come on, Nick," Jimmy sneered as he leaned back into the couch. "You think Jimmy is stupid enough to walk in here armed when such important guests come to visit?"

"Up," commanded Nick, motioning with his revolver. "Don't screw with me, Jimmy."

"Chief's got a rock up his ass this morning, boys," Jimmy stated loudly as he rose and moved to the wall. 'O.K. Chief. Search me. But don't play with my balls too long. I don't go for that shit."

Quickly and expertly, Nick frisked the gang leader, amidst the hoots and jeers encouraged by the gang leader's comments.

"Now, Chief," Jimmy resumed as he returned to the couch. "Let's get down to business. I wanna see your fucking warrant. Now."

Nick reached into an inside pocket of his vest and pulled out a folded document, tossing to Sanchez. The biker scanned the piece of paper for a moment, scowling as he read.

"Reasonable reason to believe major quantity of illicit narcotics on property?" he said incredulously, looking up at Nick. "What is this shit? Who's your informant, Nicky? Because he's fulla crap. You ain't gonna find squat in this place. Nothing. I just might sue you fuckers for harassment."

Nick stared hard at Jimmy for a moment before turning to François.

"Anything on any of these guys?" he asked.

"They all had switchblades," François replied. "Those aren't legal. Two guns. A little grass, hash and coke."

"Possession of illegal weapons and drugs," mused Nick, staring once again at Jimmy. "Take them in. All of them. We're pressing charges."

"What is this garbage, Sharp?" argued Jimmy from the couch. "Why you fucking with us like this? You're gonna bust my guys for knifes and grass? You won't have time to start the fucking paperwork, they'll be back here. Why don't you fucking leave us alone?"

Nick gazed at Jimmy without answering, waiting for the other gang members to be handcuffed and led from the house. After a moment, they were alone.

"You're wasting everybody's fucking time, Sharp," Jimmy snarled, his anger obviously growing. "You ain't gonna find anything in this fucking place. Understand?"

"That's where you're wrong, asshole," Nick replied calmly, almost gently.

He reached into his bulky protective vest, pulled out two one kilo bags of cocaine and tossed them to Sanchez. François, who had re-entered the room in the interim, came forward, throwing another bag on the couch. A third officer came in from the dining room holding two additional bags.

"You see, Jimmy," Nick continued softly. "You're wrong, asshole."

Stunned, Jimmy stared at the five bags of coke as he quietly muttered, "Motherfuckers,"

Looking up at Nick, he suddenly screamed, "MOTHERFUCKERS!" as he pulled out a revolver from between the cushions of the couch.

Long before he ever had time to get the gun clear, all three officers raised their weapons in response, firing five shots in total. Thirteen minutes after the raid had commenced, it was over and Diamond Jimmy Sanchez was dead.

* * * *

Alex "Kid" Wilson stood on the porch of the St-Sauveur residence, still fuming at having to be there. That was thanks to his brother, Chains, the high and mighty second in command, who had volunteered him for the job.

"The exposure will do you good, Kid", the senior Wilson had said. "You've got to do a job once in a while or the other guys won't respect you."

The other gang members had stood around with smirks on their faces.

Alex enjoyed being in the gang for several reasons; status, drugs, women, money. He just didn't like having to work to obtain these lifely pleasures and being Chains' little brother usually got him excused from the lowlife tasks.

Recently however, some of the other members had started bitching that the "Kid" was riding for free and this was quickly becoming unacceptable. Everybody had to do their share. This was why Kid now stood on this porch, enjoying the pleasures of the sub-zero winter.

At least he had gotten the porch. He'd made that clear as soon as they'd arrived. There was no way he'd go stand out in the woods and freeze his balls off.

As he mulled over his frustration, he noticed a man rush clumsily among the trees near the road and hide behind a massive pine. After a few seconds, the intruder dashed again, moving another ten feet, to the cover of a large rock. He raised his head a foot above the rock, looking towards the house for several seconds before dropping back into hiding. He resembled a young child playing war games, badly. Even when he attempted to hide, he was clearly visible to Kid.

Taking hold of the rifle he had slung over his back, Kid crept cautiously off to the left, taking a circular path to approach the unwelcome visitor from behind. Within in a minute, he had covered forty yards and could now clearly see the man, still crouched behind the large rock. He approached quietly, thinking of the glory coming his way. The "Kid" would show those assholes what he was made of. He would single-handedly bring this job to its conclusion.

He reached the intruder from behind just as the latter was once again attempting to peer towards the house over the rock. Pressing the gun barrel into the back of the man's neck, Kid spoke in a quiet, sure tone.

"Get up real slow, motherfucker. Real slow."

The stranger stood up, instinctively raising his hands above his head.

"Turn around, asshole," ordered Kid, backing away a couple of steps. "Watcha looking for?"

"Uh, n-nothing," stammered Jonathan. "Just looking, that's all."

"Looking for what?" Kid demanded. "Looking how you can get inside that house, maybe? We've been waiting for you, mister."

He finished his sentence, oblivious of his impending fate. From behind, Chris, armed with a heavy club improvised from a fallen limb, swung at the gang member's head. Death was immediate, the blow so forceful that Kid's body literally lifted off the ground and was projected a half dozen feet away where it slammed into a large maple tree.

"Thanks," said Jonathan as he moved towards the lifeless form.

"I owed you one," responded Chris, scanning the area to make sure they had not attracted any attention.

"Where did you learn to hit like that?" asked Jonathan, examining the messy wound on the dead biker's skull.

"Years of practice," Chris replied.

* * * *

Bryan drove through the village of St-Sauveur, feeling strangely calm. He would be back at Matt's chalet in a little under ten minutes, five if he hurried. But he was in no hurry.

He had respected the speed limit during his hour long drive, although he could have easily driven faster with little risk of getting pulled over, just by following the Saturday morning traffic; city dwellers rushing to the multitude of ski centres available to them all over the Laurentians. People whose prime concern was to get out there to breathe fresh air and pack in as many runs as they could in one day; people who read about drug traffickers and murderers in the papers and found such things horrible. He had been surrounded by such people on the drive down and had found it quite comforting, being amongst the normal, generally good people. He had not been in any rush to part company with them.

The cellular phone still wasn't functioning. He'd tried it several times on the way down but to no avail. The battery was fully charged but he couldn't get a signal. He chuckled to himself as he thought of Wayne who was probably freaking out by now, waiting for a call. Well, Wayne wouldn't have long to wait now before finding out what was going on. Bryan would be there in a few minutes and he'd bring his friend up to speed.

He wasn't sure what Wayne's next plan of action would be. All he knew was that if it wasn't absolutely brilliant, he was hopping a plane and getting the hell out. He had more than enough to retire on and frankly, he was growing tired of the cold Quebec winters.

* * * *

"Yeah, well, no doubt about it," Jonathan confirmed as he stood from Kid's body. "He's definitely dead."

"We're gonna have to dump him somewhere," said Chris as he surveyed the area. "He's too visible from the driveway and the road."

"I'll look after that," Jonathan replied, nodding. "You go and check out the house. I'll join you as soon as I can."

He picked up the dead man's rifle, slinging it by its strap over his right shoulder then hoisted the corpse over his left. He had noticed a rather deep ditch which ran alongside the road and ended just across the driveway and was certain that their latest victim would be comfortable there. As he moved off, Chris headed through the thick woods towards the house, and Sandy.

* * * *

Bryan drove up the hill, the last stretch of road before reaching the cottage. As he came around the bend, he thought he caught a glimpse of some movement behind a cluster of thick evergreens. Suddenly, it dawned on him that Barry might be here. After all, with the way Matt had been mutilated, it must have been to make him talk. A cold shiver gripped his body as he realized that he was quite possibly in extreme danger.

He slowed the vehicle as he pulled out his small .22. He wouldn't die without a fight.

* * * *

Having made his way around to the west side of the house, Chris examined the building from across the fifteen foot clearing which obviously

214

served as a parking area. He found what he was looking for, just as the blueprints had indicated; a four foot square door leading to the basement. Its usual purpose was to facilitate the bringing in of firewood. Today however, it would serve nicely as his point of entry.

* * * *

The driveway leading from the road to Matt's chalet did not run in a straight line. Rather, it zigzagged around a number of mature trees which the original owner had wished to preserve. The added benefit was intimacy as one could not really see the house from the road through the multitude of trees.

This landscaping, and the cover it offered, pleased Jonathan as he hurried across the driveway towards the ditch on the other side, loaded with the guard's body.

A sudden glint of light through the trees down the hill, followed by the rumble of an engine caught his attention. Someone was coming.

As he reached the edge of the ditch, he glimpsed the approaching silver grey vehicle through an opening amongst the heavy pines. Hurriedly, he heaved the corpse off his shoulder, catapulting it into the ditch. With barely time to turn around, he saw the Mercedes veer slowly into the driveway and come to an abrupt stop, the driver staring at him.

He approached the car, holding the rifle across his chest, the picture of an alert guard.

"Sorry, private property, Mister," he informed the driver through the partially lowered window.

"Who the fuck are you?" demanded Bryan, his small .22 concealed just below the bottom of the window, his finger on the trigger.

"Ice," Jonathan coldly replied. "Now, who the fuck are you?"

"I'm staying here for a few days," Bryan shot back.

"Are you Bryan Downey?" asked Jonathan, his tone slightly less aggressive.

"Y-yes. Yes I am," responded Bryan, relaxing a little.

"Can I see some identification, Mr. Downey," continued Jonathan. "Jimmy told us to be real careful about who we let in."

"Sure, sure," answered Bryan as he slipped his gun into his jacket pocket and pulled out his wallet. "There you go."

Jonathan gave the driver's permit a cursory glance and handed it back.

"Thanks. Sorry if I came on strong, Mr. Downey. Jimmy gave us strict orders."

"No problem," Bryan reassured him. "Better safe than sorry. What happened to the other guy that was here?"

"Jimmy sent me to replace him," replied Jonathan. "They needed him back in town for something."

"Well, good," Bryan grinned. "He was a little too much of a snot nose whiner for my taste. No problems so far this morning?"

"No sir," Jonathan answered. "We've got things under control."

"Excellent," approved Bryan. "You guys keep up the good work."

"Yessir, Mr. Downey," replied Jonathan. "You've got nothing to worry about."

* * * *

Chris scrambled across the clearing to the relative safety offered by the elevated porch which ran along the west side of the house. He quickly got to work on the lock of the firewood door but suddenly froze, straining to hear.

Sure enough, as he listened, he detected the sound of tires crunching over the frozen snow, accompanied by the rumble of an engine. He pressed himself into the corner under the porch steps, breathing into his coat to avoid making steam.

The sounds grew louder and the car suddenly appeared, stopping no more than a half dozen feet away. From where Chris sat, he could see the front left side of Bryan's Mercedes, including the first half foot of the driver's door. He had no idea if the driver, presumably Bryan, could see him.

Being careful to move as little as possible, he withdrew the heavy revolver from the holster strapped under his right arm and waited. He hoped he wouldn't have to use it for now, but had no intention of getting shot himself, at least not without a fight.

The car door opened, the driver disembarked and swung the door back shut. He took a few steps forward and stopped, scanning the woods which surrounded them. It was Bryan. Apparently satisfied with what he saw, he turned and walked back, out of sight. Within seconds, Chris heard the man's footsteps climb the staircase over his head, a key insert into a lock and the creak of hinges as a door opened and then slammed shut.

Chris breathed deeply for a moment, realizing that he had been instinctively holding his breath then returned his attention to the task at hand.

* * * *

217

"Where the fuck were you?" bellowed Wayne as Bryan entered the house. "I asked you to fucking call."

"Wayne, go screw yourself," Bryan tiredly responded, hanging his coat on a peg by the door. "Give me a fucking break. Matt and Greg are dead, O.K.? I saw their fucking bodies, not you. I tried to call you but my goddamn phone isn't working anymore. I need a drink."

He stomped over to the bar and poured himself a healthy tot of scotch as Wayne slumped heavily into the couch.

"The bastard killed them," Wayne murmured softly, shocked by this latest unfavourable turn of events.

"Yeah, the bastard killed them," Bryan mimicked. "And judging from the condition of Matt's body, he was obviously tortured, so now the bastard probably knows where we are."

"Jesus fucking Christ," Wayne cursed. "What about Greg?"

"I'm not sure if someone killed him or if the little twerp committed suicide," answered Bryan. "I found him sitting at his computer with his brains blown all over the room and a gun in his hand."

"We're gonna have to get outta here," decided Wayne.

"And then what?" challenged Bryan. "Where we gonna go from here? What's the big plan, Wayne?"

"I don't know yet," Wayne shot back. "Let me think. Maybe Jimmy can help us out."

"Well, I'm seriously considering catching a plane and getting the hell outta the country," Bryan informed his partner. "I've got enough to live on."

"Yeah, but you can have more, Bryan. Much more," replied Wayne with conviction. "Let me think a little. I'll figure something out."

"You better think quick, my friend," Bryan decisively warned. "And it better be good. Otherwise, you're on your own."

* * * *

Chris had studied the blueprints which Matt had been good enough to provide him with and had a clear image of the house's layout imprinted in his mind.

Although the shades which covered the basement windows were quite opaque, enough daylight filtered in from the sides to render his flashlight unnecessary. Considering the absence of light, he was relatively certain sure that nobody lurked in any corner.

If Matt had told the truth, and Chris was confident that he had, the only people on the property were Wayne, Bryan and the four guards; and, of course, Sandy. Since the four guards had been taken care of rather permanently, there remained only two to deal with.

He quietly and cautiously began to explore the basement, a task which would consume little time. Most of it was actually one big room, the game room in which he currently found himself, equipped with a pool table, bar, fireplace, sound system and so on. A small complete bathroom could be found in one corner towards the back of the house and the furnace room, in the other corner. Sandwiched between these two rooms was a cold room.

Considering the fact that it was windowless and had a heavy, locking door, it made an ideal place to imprison someone. Chris hoped that Sandy's captors had also believed this. Getting her safely out of the building would make the remainder of the tasks of the day so much easier.

He reached the door and gently turned the knob, praying for it to be locked but, to his dismay, it wasn't. Barring a variety of bottles, jars and the like, the room was empty which meant that Sandy was upstairs somewhere.

He'd just have to go up there and get her.

* * * *

"So? Have you come up with your master plan?" demanded Bryan.

His patience was wearing thin following several minutes of pacing and two hefty scotches.

"I haven't really been planning anything," admitted Wayne. "But I have been thinking about something."

"Well, why don't you share those thoughts," suggested Bryan, his sarcasm far from subtle.

Ignoring his colleague's tone, Wayne explained, "When we discovered that Barry was on to us, I was worried that he was working with the cops. Now, I'm really not so sure that he is."

"Why's that?" enquired Bryan, vaguely interested.

"Because the cops haven't shown up here," Wayne reasoned, "Even though Barry knows where we are. Because Matt and Greg are dead. I don't think Barry would have killed them if he was working for or with the police."

"Yeah, but we snatched his wife," reminded Bryan. "Maybe that made the guy go nuts."

"Maybe," Wayne responded doubtfully. "But presuming that Barry is the one who's been screwing with us all along, which we both believe he is, why did he kill Rick? Why did he set up Bob? Why did he switch the coke on us? We hadn't grabbed his wife then. No. I don't think the cops are in on this at all. I don't know what motivated the bastard to screw with us, but I'm sure it's just him and us."

"O.K. Great," accepted Bryan, puzzled. "So what's the point?"

"Point is, my friend, that I knew we would eventually have to deal with this guy and that his missus would serve as the bait. I just wasn't clear on when because I didn't know who was involved in this. Now I'm clear."

"And?" asked Bryan, still not quite following.

"If the cops aren't in on this, then the only problem is Barry," Wayne explained with a pained expression. "If he's gone, then nobody knows about our activities anymore."

"What about all these dead bodies?" questioned Bryan, not quite enthralled with Wayne's thoughts.

"What bodies? There's really been only one body so far. George. Who says Rick and Bob are dead? They've simply disappeared. Maybe they've been ripping off Quality Imports. We could short the inventory to support that theory. As far as Matt and Greg go, one was murdered and the other committed suicide. Hell, we had nothing to do with that. We were up here since Friday afternoon. We've got people in the village here that could vouch for that. All we have to do once we've taken care of Mr. Barry is keep our noses clean for a couple of months. Then we just pick up right where we left off."

Both men stared at each other for a moment. Bryan had to admit, the way Wayne explained it made a whole lot of sense; definitely plausible.

"O.K. What's our next step, then?" asked Bryan.

"We get that little bitch down here," snarled Wayne, "And the three of us will call her husband to suggest he get his butt over here real quick."

* * * *

From downstairs, Chris could hear the muffled voices of a discussion taking place on the main floor. As best as he could determine there were two people involved and both were male. The sounds of the conversation seemed louder when he moved towards the front of the house, leading him to believe that Bryan and Wayne were in the living room. That was good. The staircase leading up to the first floor was at the back of the house.

He started up the steps, slowly, one at a time, a small can of WD-40 ready for the hinges of the door on top. He wondered where Jonathan was. Considering Bryan's arrival without any evident panic, he figured that Jonathan had managed to make things appear normal. He hadn't known Jonathan for long but was confident that the man would be there if he needed him.

* * * *

Jonathan kept watch on the front porch, glancing inside on a regular basis. Wayne and Bryan were in the living room, deep in conversation, with the former doing most of the talking. There was no sign of Chris yet and Jonathan had no idea what his most recent consultant intended to do. However, Chris had clearly established that he was quick on his feet, able to rapidly evaluate a situation and react accordingly. Whatever he determined to be the appropriate action, Jonathan would be ready to back him up.

* * * *

Sandy was seated on the brass bed, her right wrist securely handcuffed to the railed headboard. Although she had no idea what fate the coming hours reserved for her, she felt strangely calm. Regardless of what happened to her, she knew that her captors would pay. Pay and suffer. Her husband would see to that. Her husband was the 'Vigilante'.

The door to the second floor bedroom suddenly swung open and Wayne strolled in, keys in hand.

"Come on, sweetheart," he smiled, unlocking the cuff at her wrist. "It's time to call hubby."

"Fuck you," she calmly responded. "I'm not doing anything to help you."

His smile turned to a nasty grimace as he spoke.

"You're not in any position to make decisions, bitch. Now, get your sweet ass downstairs or I'll throw it down."

He grabbed her wrist and pulled her roughly from the bed, propelling her from the room and down the stairs. Into the living room, he pushed her onto the couch before picking up the cordless phone which he shove in her face.

"Call," he ordered.

She gazed at him with a slight smile then spit at him in response.

"You little cunt," Wayne screamed, raising a hand to strike her.

"I wouldn't do that if I were you," warned Chris, his voice a deadly monotone.

Both Wayne and Bryan spun around in surprise to find Chris standing at the entrance of the hallway which led to the back of the house. The hole in the barrel of the .357 Magnum he held seemed large enough to walk into.

223

Bryan threw a glance at his jacket, hanging far away on the peg by the side door, thinking of his gun in the pocket.

"Don't try anything stupid," Chris ordered, turning his attention to the man for an instant.

Wayne, taking advantage of the slight diversion, pulled a revolver from behind his back and pressed its barrel to Sandy's head.

"Who's gonna shoot first, Barry?" he growled. "Who's the first to die?"

"My guess would be Mr. Barry," came Jonathan's voice from the front door, where he stood with his rifle trained on Chris's chest. "Put down that cannon real slow, Mister Barry. Real, real slow."

"Who the hell are you?" blurted Wayne, somewhat confused by the sudden appearance of this stranger.

"Ice," replied Jonathan as he took a step forward, his unblinking eyes fixed on Chris. "Jimmy's best, Mr. Mackinnon. Now, Mister Barry, I ain't gonna ask you again. Get that gun down on the floor or I'll blow your fucking heart out."

He took another step into the room as he raised the rifle butt to his shoulder, assuring better precision of his aim. Chris stared at him for a few seconds and then, slowly began lowering the gun, admitting defeat.

"Well, Chris," Wayne smugly taunted, lowering his revolver from Sandy's head. "Guess you're not that bright after all."

Turning to Jonathan who now stood no more than three feet from him he added, "Kill him."

Chris froze, his gun now down to waist level, as Jonathan grinned. "You got it, boss."

Claude Bouchard

With an unexpected swing, Jonathan whipped the barrel of his rifle into Wayne's face, sending the man reeling and his revolver clattering across the floor, safely out of reach. Losing his balance from the blow, Wayne fell and immediately found himself pinned to the ground by a rifle barrel leaning heavily into his throat.

"Everything O.K.?" Jonathan called out as he stared down at Wayne.

"Fine," replied Chris, his heavy handgun aimed directly at Bryan who, stunned by the sudden turn of events, remained very still.

"Good," said Jonathan, stepping back a few feet from Wayne. "Mr. Mackinnon, please roll over on your stomach and spread your arms and legs wide. Don't try anything stupid or I will kill you."

Wayne silently obeyed.

"Good boy," Jonathan continued. "Now, Mr. Downey, please come over here and lay down on your stomach next to your friend, same position."

A nervous Bryan abided by the request without a word.

"Thank you," Jonathan politely said.

He reached into a pocket of his leather jacket, extracted a small aerosol can and crouched down near the two men's heads.

"Night, boys," he pleasantly chanted as he quickly sprayed them to sleep.

Standing, he turned to Chris and Sandy who were already in each others arms.

"Why don't you two take a break and get reacquainted. I'll entertain our hosts in the meantime."

* * * *

Wayne and Bryan awoke within seconds of each other, their state of mind, a bit foggy. Each was propped up against and securely taped to one of each of the two oak support beams which ran from floor to ceiling between the living room and dining area.

As they regained their senses, they became aware of someone standing before them. Looking up, they recognized Chris, which quickly brought them completely back to reality.

"Gentlemen, nice to have you back," said Chris, his smile charming but his gaze deadly. "I couldn't leave without saying goodbye."

The two stared up at him but uttered no reply. The several layers of tape covering their mouths prevented them to do so.

"While you were sleeping, I had a chat with my wife," Chris continued. "I was quite interested in knowing how you gentlemen had treated her during her stay. Although she was understandably frightened by the whole ordeal, she has assured me that you did not harm her and, for that, I extend my thanks."

He paused for a moment, looking from one man to the other, before pursuing.

"Over the years, I have earned the reputation of being honest and straight-forward, a man of my word. I promised you no pain if you didn't harm Sandy and I will keep my promise."

Turning towards the dining table behind him, he pointed to a small digital clock which read 10:43.

"At precisely eleven, this clock will transmit a signal. We have placed explosives in strategic locations in the house, armed with detonators which will be triggered by the signal. The explosion will be so massive, gentlemen, that your death will be instantaneous. I promise you will feel no pain."

226

With these as his final words, he stepped through the front door to join Sandy and Jonathan, who waited in the Jeep Grand Cherokee which Jonathan had conveniently obtained for the day's activities. They drove off, heading south for home.

As they embarked onto the Laurentian autoroute, they heard and felt a sudden rumbling in the distance behind them. The clock in the Jeep's dashboard read 11:00.

Chapter 20 - Sunday, February 2, 1997

Dave McCall awoke at 6:15, which was considered sleeping in by his standards. He quietly climbed out of bed, careful not to wake Cathy. They had gotten in late the night before, following a lovely dinner and an evening of dancing which Dave had proposed in order smooth over the previous morning's silly spat.

He padded to the kitchen to get the coffee going, used the bathroom and then headed to the front door for the morning paper. Due to their evening out, he had missed the news and he liked to keep abreast of current events.

He returned to the kitchen to get some coffee before settling down to read. As he dropped the paper on the table in passing, the front page headline caught his attention. Any articles related to crime naturally piqued his interest and he forgot about his coffee as he started to read.

RCMP CRUSH DRUG IMPORT RING
AND "ACES OF DEATH"

by Ron Henderson

Following months of intense investigation, the RCMP, assisted by officers of the QPP, closed in on a major narcotics importation and distribution ring yesterday, announced Nicholas Sharp, Director of the RCMP detachment for the Province of Quebec.

Thanks to tips from informants and a series of surveillance operations which spanned a period of some eighteen months, an undercover team, headed by Sharp, was able to confirm cocaine and heroin imports from Columbia and Thailand.

The masterminds behind the complex import network are suspected to have used their employer, Quality Imports of Laval, as the cover and means to their operation. Unbeknownst to Charles Peterson, owner and president of Quality Imports, the drugs were allegedly included within regular shipments of merchandise brought into the country by the company.

Also suspected to be involved in the drug import scheme were two customs officials, one employee of Rapid Forwarders, a local customs broker as well as legal counsel to the infamous "Aces of Death" motorcycle gang which is also alleged to be involved, handling the distribution of the narcotics.

Having accumulated sufficient evidence to crack the network, the authorities proceeded with a series of raids yesterday morning during which dozens were arrested and sizeable quantities of illicit drugs and weapons were seized. Two died, including Diamond Jimmy Sanchez, head of the Aces of Death.

Interestingly enough, of the six Q.I. employees suspected to be overseeing the narcotic imports operation two have not been seen for several days while the bodies of the other four were found yesterday at various locations.

Data obtained from the personal computer of Q.I.'s Greg Pierce, who was found dead at his Laval home from an apparent suicide, indicates that relations with the Aces of Death had grown more than tense following several shipments of phoney cocaine to the bikers. It is suspected that a war may have developed between the two groups. This is supported by the discovery of six bodies in St-Sauveur late yesterday morning following a powerful explosion at a cottage, owned by Matthew Roth, also employed by Q.I., whose badly mutilated body was found in his Laval home.

Of the six bodies found in St-Sauveur, four were known members of the Aces of Death. The other two were Wayne MacKinnon and Bryan Downey, both employed by Q.I. and allegedly involved in the narcotics import scam. Police suspect that the deaths were the result of an attempted settling of accounts between the two groups.

A neighbour to the Roth cottage in St-Sauveur informed police that he saw a black Jeep Grand Cherokee leave the residence shortly before the explosion occurred. Police suspect that the vehicle was that of Robert Rivard, also employed by Q.I. and presumed to be involved in the drug operation. Rivard, according to Peterson of Q.I., is on vacation in Mexico since Thursday, although authorities have not been able to locate him to date, nor find any record of his leaving the country. Police suspect that Rivard may still be in the area, accompanied by Richard Beauchamp, also of Q.I., reported missing since Tuesday.

Dave put down the paper in a daze. Maybe Cathy had been right. Maybe something had happened to Chris or Sandy. He swore to himself for not having listened as he rushed to the phone. Frantically, he punched in the Barrys' home number, waiting impatiently as it rang.

"Hello?" answered Chris's sleepy voice.

"Chris! You're home," exclaimed Dave, surprised, but pleased.

"Where else would you expect me to be this early in the morning?" mumbled Chris. "What time is it?"

"Nearly six-thirty," Dave sheepishly replied. "Listen, I'm sorry if I woke you. I was just worried about you guys since I learned what was happening at Quality Imports."

"What? What's happening at Quality Imports?" asked Chris, still sleepy and obviously confused. "What are you talking about, Dave?"

"You can read about it in the paper. Sorry I woke you, Chris," Dave apologized. "Go back to sleep and give me a call later, O.K.?"

"I will go back to sleep," Chris agreed with a yawn. "But since I have you on the phone, why don't you people come over for dinner tonight?"

"Well, if Sandy's not feeling well," Dave started.

"Sandy has never felt better," Chris interrupted. "See you later. Goodnight."

Dave replaced the receiver in its cradle as Cathy padded into the kitchen, yawning.

"Who are you talking to at this hour?" she asked, squinting in the light.

"Chris," replied Dave, grinning. "And for your information, he and Sandy are fine, just like I told you."

* * * *

Chris and Sandy were comfortably seated in the den watching television when the doorbell rang.

"You sure you're O.K. with this?" Chris asked as they headed towards the front door. "You have your story straight?"

"It's a little too late now anyways, wouldn't you say?" his wife replied sweetly before opening the door to greet their dinner guests.

"Hey there," they chorused as they ushered Cathy and Dave in from the cold.

A round of hugs and kisses took place during which Cathy complimented Chris on how elegant he looked wearing a turtle-neck sweater.

"It's to hide the hickeys Sandy gave me," he kidded, thinking of the bruises left by the gorilla's attempt at strangulation less than thirty-six hours earlier.

"So I guess you're feeling better?" an ever-concerned Cathy asked Sandy as the latter took her coat.

"I'm great," reassured Sandy. "It was just a temporary thing, something that didn't agree with me. Come on. Let's go to the kitchen and let these two catch up on sports and stuff."

"I was worried about you," Cathy persisted as they walked off, "Especially when I couldn't reach you yesterday."

"Oh, we were visiting with some acquaintances of Chris' up north yesterday..." were Sandy's words as the two women departed, causing Chris to involuntarily smile.

"What's so funny?" asked Dave as Chris motioned his guest towards the den.

"Women and how they worry," Chris candidly replied.

"Tell me about it," stated Dave as Chris tossed him a beer from the fridge at the bar. Although, I have to admit that when I read the paper this morning, I was concerned."

"Yeah, quite a story," Chris agreed as they relaxed into a couple of comfortable leather easy chairs. "I spoke to Peterson earlier and he's quite shocked, poor guy. I'm gonna give him a hand to keep the place running until he gets himself some replacement management."

"You think this might affect his business?" Dave enquired. "You can't consider that this was the best kind of free publicity a company can get."

"I asked Charlie about that," Chris responded. "He told me that he's already received calls from a number of larger clients offering help, sympathy and their full support. No, I don't think that this is gonna hurt him."

Dave remained quiet for a moment, hesitant to even ask the question. Finally, he mustered up the courage and simply blurted it out.

Claude Bouchard

"Chris, you had *no* idea that any of this was going on? I mean, I know you were just there for a couple of weeks, but still. Didn't you notice anything out of the ordinary?"

"Can't tell you more than you already know," Chris shrugged nonchalantly. "I was just a consultant."

The two men fell silent as they turned their attention to the news on the television, first watching a report on the bombing of a farm in Columbia, followed by another from Thailand regarding an explosion at a clothing manufacture and the destruction of a bar known to be a criminal hang-out.

Made in the USA
Lexington, KY
07 December 2012